Walking Evil

Mark St. Germain

For my canine soulmate, Sarge

While the events in this book are drawn from my life, some iden-
tities have been changed. The dogs, however, have not been altered save surgically.

ADVANCE PRAISE FOR
Walking Evil

"Walking Evil is a marvelously written, highly entertaining book about a very bad dog, a very good dog, a parrot, and their human family. If you have ever loved a good dog, or a bad dog, or a fast-talking parrot, you will fall in love with Walking Evil. It is the perfect antidote to these hard strange times."

Abigail Thomas, author *of A Three Dog Life*

"Without the ironic charm of the author's voice, this might have been another typical horror story of a man locked in battle with a dog from hell. Instead, our droll, wise-cracking narrator delights us with a bitter-sweet, often hilarious tale of a sympathetic pro-tagonist caught in the eternal triangle of man, wife, and diabolical canine."

Billy Collins U.S. Poet Laureate

Table of Contents

PROLOGUE

Timmy had Lassie, Dorothy had Toto, Turner had Hooch.

I had Evil.

Those of you expecting a heartwarming story of a man and his dog should now reconsider. The phrase "unconditional love" goes unmentioned here. *Walking Evil* is what happens when man's best friend becomes his worst enemy. If you decide to read on, I suggest having a copy of *Old Yeller* or *The Poky Little Puppy* nearby for comfort. And, please, don't leave this book around for children to read. The last thing I want to cause is preschooler panic at the sight of every dog in the neighborhood.

There are countless magnificent dogs, we all know that. I had one named Sarge, who tried his best to pretend Evil didn't exist.

It was Evil who challenged my belief that our relationship with dogs is always one of mutual, tender trust. Trust that a canine looks at their person as a loyal caregiver. Not a master, because we'd prefer not to think of it that way. We want our relationship with our dog to be one of equals, or as equal as a relationship between a *Homo sapiens* and a *Canis lupus* can be, leaving four-footed mobility and a tail aside.

Walking Evil is a cautionary tale, but if you need reassurance that this dark tunnel has a light in the distance, consider that, since I am here writing it, I am still alive.

Sorry, but that's about as optimistic as it gets.

"Look out for the dogs, look out for the evildoers."
Philippians 3:2

CHAPTER ONE

THE DAWN OF EVIL

"Evil?"

No response. The World O' Pups trainer on the store's loudspeaker tried again, louder this time. "Will Evil come to the training area? Calling Evil to the training area." I looked at my wife, Emma, sitting beside me in the Puppy Parents Lounge. "He's calling her," I said.

My wife rolled her eyes at what she assumed was a pointed joke before realizing I was serious.

"It's *Evie!*" she shouted, jumping to her feet and pulling her uncooperative puppy by its leash across the polished store floor.

In my heart, I knew the trainer had made no mistake. He might think he'd read the name wrong, but he'd soon realize, with the instincts of his beast-taming gut, that he had got it right the first time. I hadn't been at home when Emma and our daughter Becca named her. They had picked up this rescue puppy at a shelter near our home in Woodstock, New York, while I was in Massachusetts working on a new play at the Barrington Stage Company.

Had I been there to influence their decision to get a second dog, or even this particular dog, there's a chance that we would all be living much different, much happier, lives today.

"Guess what we named her?" Becca asked. "Clue: *The Garden of Eden.*" I picked up the puppy curled in her lap. Up to now, this tiny Labrador–greyhound mix with a shining black coat had completely ignored me while somehow making it obvious. She demonstrated that now by squirming out of my arms and barking to be returned to the protection of her sisterhood.

"The Garden of Eden?" I repeated. "Okay. Satan?"

Becca laughed. For the first time, the dog turned her attention to me. It was also the first time I'd ever seen any animal demonstrate disdain.

Was this when the war began?

Our son Martin was away at college, and Becca was spending her last weeks at home before leaving to teach English as a second language in Taiwan. Emma had convinced herself that with her second child leaving the house, it made perfect sense to replace our daughter with a dog she could call her own. Luckily, Becca didn't make this connection. Emma was certain that our first dog, Sarge, a sad-eyed black Labrador retriever and hound mix, would be as excited as she was with the idea.

Sarge was the first dog I ever had. In my childhood, I was severely allergic to dogs, cats, and live Christmas trees. Put a live dog, cat, and Christmas tree together and the fast-rising red bumps on my arms sensed their presence a mile away.

The nearest my brother, sister, and I came to having a pet were a finch and an alligator. My brother, Paul, has never forgiven me for unknowingly plopping down on a chair in our bedroom shortly after his finch did. The alligator's end was more mysterious. Our grandparents, returning from an annual drive to Florida, stopped at a roadside stand and brought home a tiny baby alligator as a souvenir for us.

He was six inches long, if that.

We were diligent about feeding him and changing his water. His home grew from a dish to a fishbowl and, finally, to a plastic tank about five by three feet. His daily diet came to include small fish we caught from a local stream. He showed his appreciation by growing, and our parents' concern increased with every foot he grew.

One weekend my grandparents took us for a short vacation to Long Beach Island, New Jersey. We returned to find our alligator had vanished and his tank was drained. Our dry-eyed father explained that he had mysteriously died of an undetected illness in the three days we were gone.

I wish I could remember the poor reptile's name. It wasn't Lucky.

Years later, then, my children grew up with fake evergreens and non-hairy pets. We had iguanas and didn't realize they grew to the size of their environment, resulting in their own separate and enormous pens. We had hamsters, birds of all kinds, and our family favorite, Carmen, the orange spotted tortoise. I'd like to think Carmen enjoyed us, as well.

We knew that Carmen liked television, particularly *Lassie*, which we watched every morning before rushing the kids to school moments before the bell rang. Carmen sat with us on the living room rug and not only faced the TV screen but moved only during commercials.

When the rest of the family was out, Carmen would slowly make her way to the desk where I was working and sit by my feet. When I went downstairs, she waited patiently on the top step for me to return. In her too-brief life, she only once had to go to the vet, when she stopped eating. An X-ray revealed we had found the missing earring Emma was looking for.

At a tortoise's pace, Carmen eventually returned the earring after we sorted through a few days of tortoise muck.

Sarge, like Evil, was also a rescue. When I was shooting a documentary about the unusual relationship between celebrities and their dogs—more later—I told our consulting veterinarian, Amy Attas, that I wished I had grown up without allergies and with a pet instead. She looked at me oddly, asking if I had experienced breathing problems during the past weeks of filming. When I told her I hadn't, her tone changed as if she was addressing someone who instantly had dropped dozens of IQ points.

"Why don't you go into a room with a dog, close the door, and sit there for an hour to see if you have a reaction?" So I did. The room turned out to be a school gymnasium in White Plains, New York. Emma, Becca, and I attended an adoption day with the intent to determine the dander's effect on my rashes and respiratory system. It would be a field trip only, we agreed; no dog shopping yet.

Despite being surrounded by dogs and their dander, I didn't suffer a bump or a sniffle. My breathing remained normal. I must have outgrown my allergy. We started looking at the dogs with real interest. For the first time in my life, and my children's, we could have a furry pet.

There were no individual cages, only a basketball court where over a hundred dogs of all kinds ran back and forth, inspecting their potential adopters. One dog, a black Labrador Retriever mix, stopped before us, looking up expectantly. We petted him and continued our walk around the gym. Becca was hoping to adopt a puppy, despite the fact that she'd be away at school while we would be training it.

We ruffled the fur of other dogs that presented themselves for affection. It wasn't long before we realized that no matter how long we continued looking, this black Labrador retriever would be at our side. He had adopted us. Even Becca, who had wanted a puppy, was charmed. His tail wagged every time we made eye contact, and he was the embodiment of gentleness.

Devora, the woman running the event, assured us that she could already see a strong connection between dog and family. Calculated or not, it confirmed our decision that this was our dog. She called our wonderful neighbor, Diane, whose house was a few animals short of Noah's ark, to get a reference on us. No answer. Leaving a message, Devora told us we could come back in two days if we passed scrutiny.

"His name is Sarge," she informed us. We told Sarge we'd return, but he continued to follow us and had to be restrained as we reached the gym's exit.

"Wait!" Devora caught up with us. She had just been called back by our neighbor. "You're approved! And it looks like Sarge is ready to go."

Without a leash, Sarge walked with us to our car and hopped into the back seat the minute the door was open. He was ours and we were his. He walked through our front door that day as if he was home. And he was.

Sarge had a gentle disposition. He would greet visitors by approaching them, waiting to be acknowledged, and if he weren't, he would simply return to whatever dog activity he was about. He seemed to know when we would return home and be waiting for us. He'd be hugged or petted, and he was happy. So were we. He was incredibly patient with children and, most remarkably, Evie/Evil, who wanted him to match her manic energy. Sarge just didn't. When she wore herself out jumping all over him, Sarge just quietly moved on.

When we adopted Sarge he had a hairless ring around his neck. It was caused, we were told, by the constant rubbing of a chain that was fastened around him. Sarge was brought to New York State in a truck picking up dogs from a pound down south that had a strict policy regulating the length of time a dog could live there. If the strays were found on the street, they were given a month to be adopted before being euthanized. Bizarrely, if someone brought their pet in, claiming they could no longer take care of it, that dog was given only two weeks before being destroyed. The reasoning? If somebody didn't like their dog enough to keep him, there was probably something wrong with the animal.

Sarge had a previous owner or owners, that was clear by the damage from the chain. We found out more about two years after he joined us. We brought Sarge to a vet because he was eating less. An X-ray was suggested. While the X-ray didn't spot his problem, which was subsequently treated with antibiotics, the imaging revealed something more troubling.

Sarge was full of buckshot. Because of the amount of it, the vet believed that the buckshot wasn't the result of a onetime misfire but that he had been shot at regularly. Target practice?

Fortunately, he showed no signs that it physically affected him. More amazingly, it didn't affect his warm, affectionate disposition. Sarge had been chained up, shot at, and discarded, but still trusted, even loved people.

To put a fine point on it, Sarge was the best dog ever born into this world. He was accepted instantly by our extended family and friends, and the only bad feelings were those of Martin and Becca, who were annoyed that I hadn't realized they could have had a dog years ago.

Once Evil arrived, they weren't so sure.

One of the advantages of getting a second dog, Emma insisted, was that Sarge would have a companion to play with. It would keep him young. When Evil arrived, Sarge had been part of our family for six years. With his age guesstimated at three or so years when we got him, that would put him at nine, or roughly fifty human years.

True, Evil did give Sarge exercise by keeping him on the run. Evil's idea of playing was to jump up on his back and ride him around the house or show how quickly she could devour his dinner and hers before Sarge lumbered into the kitchen.

It was obvious from the start that Evil was no saintly Sarge. But at first, we blithely believed her unruly behavior could be remedied. World O' Pups had a weekly training class and Emma faithfully took Evie there. At the end of the four-week course, my wife came proudly home with a picture of Evil wearing a graduation cap and looking extremely put out.

"She passed obedience class?" I asked, failing to hide my disbelief.

"Yes. She did."

"Did *all* the dogs graduate?"

"Why would that matter?"

"Got it. Can she sit?"

"Not yet."

"Beg? Roll over? Stay? Heel?"

"No."

"Did she learn anything?"

Emma hesitated. She was well aware that the relationship between Evil and me was a rocky one, with neither of us likely to helm the other's booster club.

"Well, what *I* learned is she's an incredible runner," she offered. "It's probably the greyhound/Labrador mix."

"How do you know that?"

"She pulled so hard she broke her leash, then outran the trainer and the store manager chasing her around the mall. Didn't you, girl?" Emma patted her while Evil gave me what looked like a dog smirk.

Evil had become a serious discipline problem, a threat to my very livelihood and possessions. When Evil had earlier pulled all the books off the lowest shelves of my office and munched each one democratically, I was determined to stop this behavior in its tracks. She was devouring *The Plays of Eugene O'Neill* and heading for my own mementos.

I often wrote scripts about historical figures, and over the years, I had collected their autographs. The collection was built slowly, due to the price of these important particular signatures. Often, the value of the autograph exceeded the royalties I received from the work.

I had written a screenplay about Melvin Purvis, the FBI agent who captured John Dillinger, and acquired a letter from Purvis framed with his picture. After *Camping with Henry and Tom*, a play based on a camping trip taken by Thomas Edison, Henry Ford, and their unlikely companion President Warren G. Harding, the only autograph I could afford was Harding's. I consoled myself with the thought that even one autograph put me in the circle of the most dedicated Warren G. Harding collectors.

On my wish list was an autograph of Sigmund Freud. I had written a play, *Freud's Last Session*, about an imagined meeting between the founder of psychoanalysis and C. S. Lewis shortly before Freud's suicide. For that especially valuable signature, I'd have to wait until some Freud enthusiast in Hollywood decided to film the play and give me a healthy sum to buy a Freud signature.

Evil had destroyed only one autograph, that of Yoko Ono. My play *Ears on a Beatle* followed two FBI men assigned to monitor John Lennon and Yoko Ono in 1980, when Richard Nixon and

J. Edgar Hoover were eager to deport them before they returned to political activism. The play was successfully produced, and I acquired an autograph, a kind gift from Yoko Ono herself.

Whether because of the colors of Yoko's bright postcard, the fact that it was personally addressed to me, or Evil's belief that Yoko broke up the Beatles, Evil targeted it for obliteration.

At the scene of the crime, I got to my knees, took her collar in my hand, and spoke firmly, only inches from her face. "No! Wrong! Bad girl!"

I had heard of owners training their dogs not to do their business in the house by rubbing their noses in it. *Cruel*, I thought, and definitely too gross. But holding up a mangled postcard in front of Evil's nose to illustrate her misdeeds seemed appropriate and should teach her a connection between bad behavior and punishment.

Evil eyed its shredded remains as coolly as she did me. I repeated my scolding several times, then released her and watched as she turned from me and went calmly on her way. Her way, I quickly discovered, was to make another visit to my office and drop what seemed a larger than puppy-sized load in front of my desk.

This didn't happen once or twice. It happened every time the Dog Who Must Not Be Named and I clashed.

"It's spite," I told Emma. "Every time I try to discipline her, she comes into my office and dumps in the exact same place. I sit down to write and there it is, in front of my eyes and nose. She does it deliberately. There's no other explanation. Maybe she really *is* evil."

"Or maybe she's a critic," Emma suggested.

She smiled, at least.

"The devil's agents may be of flesh and blood, may they not?"
Sherlock Holmes, *"The Hound of the Baskervilles"*

CHAPTER TWO

PRE-EVIL

I first thought of dogs as a subject while I was walking on a picket line for the Writers Guild of America, East in 2007. Twelve thousand television and film writers went out on strike for a fair share of the profits made by major studios. The strike lasted for 100 days. The WGA East mobilized teams of writers to march in front of New York City TV and film production offices. It was a frozen, wet winter, but the membership came through. I made some new friends and met several writers I admired.

The Teamsters Union marched with us in solidarity. One teamster, a solid man in his sixties, told me we were wasting our time marching in circles. "You think those people care?" he asked, gesturing toward the corporate headquarters we were picketing. "Hell, no," he answered himself. "You want to get their attention, let's go in there and start throwing chairs through the windows."

It never came to that. Part of me was disappointed. One of the frequent presences around the picket line was a dog trainer. He entertained us, putting his dog through his repertoire of tricks and, for a finale, gave his mutt a big wet kiss. After seeing this for the first time, I made sure I turned away before their inter-species smooch. Shivering in the cold is one thing, shivering at the sight of someone enthusiastically tongue kissing a canine is something else.

What the man and his dog did was to make me think of dogs, something I usually didn't. I had been rewriting a script of Richard

Gere's that was later released as *Hachi*, inspired by the true story of a Japanese Akita, Hachiko, going daily to the train station to meet his master for nine years after his master died.

I remember sitting in Richard's kitchen for the first time and talking about the script. He was friendly, yet formal.

When Richard's dog, Billie, ran into the kitchen, the atmosphere changed instantly. He was on the floor, wrestling with him and talking to his dog as if he were seeing a beloved long-lost friend for the first time in years. Following that, conversation with me was instantly warmer.

It wasn't the first time I saw this reaction when a celebrity was joined by their pet. Working with Glenn Close, I saw a transformation in her when her dogs, Jake and Bill, joined her. At the time I wasn't sure what changed. Today I would say that love entered the room.

But not then. Dogs were dogs. I liked them better than cats, but not as much as having a burger and beer at Fat Mike's. I couldn't understand this naked, almost embarrassing connection between people and their pets.

Most summers, I spend time at the Barrington Stage Company in the Berkshires, a theater co-founded by Artistic Director Julianne Boyd and Managing Director Susan Sperber in 1995. My relationship with Julie goes back even further to her producing my first New York off-Broadway showcase of my play *The Collyer Brothers at Home*.

Working on a new play at Barrington, I got a call from Chris Invar, an actor and director with whom I've often worked. He asked me to drop by his apartment after rehearsal.

Chris had a German shepherd mix named Jack whom he'd raised from a pup. Jack was now seventeen years old, two years older than the average life span for a mixed breed dog. Trying to walk Jack around the yard demonstrated how enfeebled he was. His back legs were nearly paralyzed. The dog was clearly exhausted, eager to return to his home and sleep.

"I don't know what to do," Chris said. "He's hurting, I see that. But I can't let him go. Just the thought." Chris stopped, a catch in his voice. "What do you think?"

Seeing the pain both Chris and Jack were in, I gave my opinion. Chris had to put the dog out of his misery, no matter how miserable he felt doing it. Chris agreed. I'm sure he already knew it. It took him two trips to the vet. On his first he sat on the floor of the waiting room playing with Jack, then left before he was called in to the doctor.

Though I sympathized, there was a small and cynical part of me that thought Chris was an actor overacting. Yes, of course he'd miss his dog, but it was the right thing to do. He'd get over it. He was treating his dog like a member of his family. Such a bond was inconceivable to me when I began walking in circles with other strikers during the constant snowstorms and droning protest chants.

During the strike, writers could not write a word for hire. That meant that they were free to do anything else so long as it didn't involve putting pen to paper.

That day, thinking of the Dog-Smoocher, Richard Gere, and Glenn Close, an idea came to me. The relationship between public figures and their dogs seemed to be a unique one. What causes it, and is there any difference between that bond or the emotional connection between John and Dog Doe?

I couldn't write about it, but I could make a film.

I brought the idea to Daryl Roth, a veteran producer responsible for many acclaimed Broadway and off-Broadway hits, whom

I'd worked with previously. There was another reason to go to Daryl. I had seen her with her own dog, treating him with the same affection she'd show a beloved child.

We decided to co-produce a documentary, *My Dog, an Unconditional Love Story*. I had directed plays before, but never a movie. It was not only a rewarding experience; it was an educational journey akin to attending film school.

At the same time, it was a learning experience to study the strong bonds between our interviewees and their dogs. Lynn Redgrave decided to adopt a dog after she was diagnosed with cancer. She wanted to care for someone beside herself, and a dog would force her to exercise, taking it for walks daily. Greg Louganis, former Olympian, found comfort in his dogs when going through a deep depression. Instead of training divers, he decided to train dogs.

"Divers don't always listen to you. Dogs do."

Actress Didi Conn and her husband, Academy Award– winning composer David Shire, adopted their son, Danny, as an infant. Concerned about his development, they visited a number of doctors before discovering Danny was autistic. Danny was averse to their touch, a not uncommon result of autism. Understandably, it caused them great anguish. Only when they bought a sheepdog puppy into their lives did Danny begin making contact with another creature. Danny began to play with the sheepdog, eventually sleeping with the dog for company. Their interaction opened a deeper level of physical communication with his parents. It was impossible not to be moved hearing Didi remember the first time Danny gave her a hug.

Isaac Mizrahi described his dog, Harry, as his best friend, "the only person who doesn't want something from me." He was told by a psychic that both he and Harry had been together in a past life as nuns in Spain.

"I totally believe it," Isaac told us, laughing.

US Poet Laureate Billy Collins cherished the bond between him and his dog, who "follows me around like a slow-witted cousin." Sitting on his front steps on a beautiful summer day, Billy described heaven as a place where mere cats wrote prose, and only the dogs wrote poetry.

From early in the filming it was clear there was a magic here. With the organizational help of Nicole Davenport and the editing guidance of Steve Heffner, we completed the film and successfully premiered it.

Adopting Sarge was the real reward that came from it.

And then came Evil.

"I have given a name to my pain and call it 'dog.'"
Friedrich Nietzsche

CHAPTER THREE

IN THE COMPANY OF EVIL

It was no surprise that Emma resented my using the name "Evil." She had used the same adjective previously to describe Charlie, another creature in our family's animal kingdom.

Charlie, the African Grey parrot I named after Darwin, was a gift from Emma—one she would rue giving. I had become fascinated with parrots and visited a parrot store in the area every time I was in its vicinity. I'm not sure where the impulse came to own one. Doctor Doolittle's conversations with his macaw, Polynesia? More likely a long-ago Pirate's Day in Tuckerton during a Jersey Shore summer. Regardless, I was bitten, and was about to be many more times again.

Charlie sits near me as I write this, momentarily still. If I were to get a phone call, he'd lean forward on his perch, primed to join in the conversation. When I'd say "Hello," he'd say the same. When I'd laugh, he'd laugh along with me, and, since he imitates my voice, it would sound as if I were laughing with myself. I've gotten to blocking it out, but a Lutheran pastor friend once stopped our phone chat to take a deep breath and ask, "When are you getting rid of that fucking bird?"

I raised Charlie from the age of two weeks, feeding him with a dropper. Most African Greys are one-person birds, and as I was Charlie's mother figure, the bond was immediate.

The results were predictable. Charlie wanted undivided attention and bristled at the presence of my wife, my children, or anyone else who wanted even a moment of my time. Parrots are beautiful, smart, and long-lived. Very long-lived. Charlie will easily outlive me, with African Greys living on average forty to sixty years. That's just one—and there are many—of the concerns any potential parrot owner should consider before adopting. Beside the financial costs of feeding and medical care, parrots are social, needing to be a part of your life.

The question of where Charlie will go when I'm gone myself is still unresolved. Emma, Martin, and Becca have their own answers, their most popular being to open a window, bring Charlie to it, and wave goodbye.

What they haven't considered is that Charlie would come back.

On the rare times that Charlie managed to escape his cage when it was put outside for him to enjoy the summer air, I would hear a knock on the front or side door. I'd look out, see no one, and hear the sound again. On the ground, Charlie was impatiently knocking on the door with his beak, demanding to be let in.

After having Charlie for several years, wings clipped, Charlie would sit on a branch of a tree in our backyard while I'd read. We'd done this dozens of times with no problem. Charlie would be happy to go outside and just as happy to jump on my finger and return to his cage.

One afternoon this went badly awry. Charlie rested peacefully until he heard a car's backfire that sounded like a cannon shot. Frightened, he flew into our neighbor's yard, sat on the grass, and waited for me come to rescue him. Instead, our neighbor's dog got there first. Fleeing as he barked, Charlie scuttled under the family van for protection. The dog ignored my shouting and began crawling on his belly to reach Charlie. Charlie weighed his options, hopped in the other direction from under the van, then flapped his clipped wings and, with panicked power, took to the air, flying across the street and into the unknown acres of woodland beyond it.

Gone. I went into the wood calling after him, distributed "Lost Parrot" posters, and spent the rest of the day watching the skies. No Charlie. As night fell, so did my hopes. *How can a bird who has never been in the wild survive?* There were hawks in the air and plenty of hungry animals on the forest floor.

The next morning it was Emma's turn to rise early and drive Becca to school. Her shouts from the first floor woke me, and I was at the top of the stairs as she called again, "Come down! Hurry!"

I followed her outside. Sitting on a small tree planted to the right of the porch was Charlie. He seemed as happy to see me as I was to see him.

"I can't believe it," I gushed. "Charlie came home!"

"He sure did," Emma conceded without any detectable enthusiasm.

"How did he find his way?"

"He had help," she said. "When Becca and I were leaving, we saw Charlie flying toward the house with two blackbirds."

"Were they chasing him?"

"No, they flew with him, one on each side."

I was amazed. "They guided him in?"

"When Charlie got close enough, they veered off. He landed on the tree and sat here waiting for you."

Inspecting Charlie closer, I saw there was something different about him. His metal band of identification, put on him at birth, was no longer around his leg. I pointed this out to Emma, who shrugged.

"He chewed it off, or one of the other birds did." "Can you imagine it?" I asked.

"Chewing off the band?"

19

"No. The party last night that Charlie and the crows had."

Nothing Charlie could ever do would change my family's feelings about him. As if knowing that, he worked hard at being dislikeable, screeching at the sight of them, imitating their voices, and repeating words and phrases he had overheard, punctuated with shrill parrot calls and whistles.

"Mark. Mark! MARK! MARK!" "No biting!" Where's Jack? FLOYD? FLOYD!" (Who the hell was Floyd?)

"STOP IT!" "Becca?" "Becca!" "GODDAMN BIRD!" (spoken in my son Martin's voice), "GO AWAY!" "I SAID NO BITING! Good Charlie! Good bird! See you later! Good night, Charlie." He also crooned an off-key version of the first verse of the Beatles' "*Blackbird.*"

After only one visit by a Cuban friend who flattered his red tail feathers, Charlie began replacing his "hellos" with "hola!" All this and his imitation of the phone ringing, water being poured, coughs, sneezes, and even the flush of a toilet got him the attention upon which he thrived.

Out of his cage, Charlie swooped down on anyone entering the room without cautiously scouting his location. His battle plan would be to climb down from his perch, walk stealthily across the floor toward his unsuspecting victim, and then bite their toes or their ankles, bare flesh preferred.

When Sarge first appeared on the scene, Charlie was overjoyed to find a new victim. He quickly learned to bark, the sound of which would lure an excited Sarge to his cage, muzzle pressed against the bars, where Charlie would lunge at him, trying to bite his nose. When Sarge finally understood he was being set up, Charlie went to plan B. With a perfect imitation of my voice, Charlie would call "Sarge! Sarge!" and Sarge would come from wherever he was in the house to Charlie. He'd stare, confused, wondering where I was. Had I shrunk enough to be calling from within the parrot's cage? Was I hiding in his food dish? Inevitably, he would move in for a closer look. With an attack squawk, Charlie would make his kamikaze dive at the dog.

Evil's arrival called for revised battle plans. Immediately, bird and dog sized each other up as a threat to their post of house warlord. Charlie quickly learned Evil's name and simulated my voice to call her. Evil approached the cage warily, sat on her haunches, and growled. Charlie quickly learned to growl back. Evil barked. Charlie barked.

I let Charlie out of his cage as much as possible. He would sit on his perch, making comments throughout the day as he observed everything around him. "Hello," he greeted anyone entering the room, and called out, "See you later!" when they left. I tried to keep him continually in my sight.

But sometimes I was distracted. If Sarge was in the room sleeping, Charlie would slide down from his perch, pad over to him, and bite his tail. Sarge would rise up and run, Charlie would laugh—"Agh! Agh! Agh!"—and I'd put him back in his cage, scolding him for his unacceptable behavior. Reportedly, African Greys are as intelligent as a four-year-old, but Charlie never learned the word "no!"

With Sarge being such an easy mark, Charlie expected the same pooch panic from Evil. On the first day he spotted her sleeping, Charlie quietly descended and approached. But only a beak away from success, Evil, having feigned sleep, jumped to her feet and plunged after him. Charlie scuttled across the wooden floor, too startled to fly.

I caught up to them as Evil cornered Charlie, whose squawks had become squeaks. Returning the grateful parrot to his cage, both of us knew his reign of terror was over. There was a new law in town, and her name was Evil.

"Cry Havoc! And let slip the dogs of war!"
Shakespeare, *Julius Caesar*

CHAPTER FOUR

EVIL IN BED

The first thing we did after bringing Sarge home was to take out a second mortgage and visit the nearest pet store. Dog food, collar, leash, feeding bowls, grooming brush, tick and flea meds, and poop bags went into the shopping cart. Several books on dog owning. We needed a second cart for the dog toys. Our biggest purchase, size wise, was a dog bed big enough for him.

We decided to put it in the kitchen, the hub of with our home. I spent time patting the bed, telling Sarge excitedly how soft and comfortable it was while he looked at me quizzically. Giving up that approach, I tried putting treats in the bed, which he simply picked up and brought to another area of the kitchen. Finally, I lay down on the bed myself, stretching out, yawning, then curling up contentedly. Sarge walked over for a closer look, licked my head, and left for the living room. I realized I had just been tucked in.

That night, when we went up to bed, Sarge followed. He had no interest in sleeping in the kitchen or on a dog bed. Instead, he stretched out on the rug at the foot of ours. Fine. He, and we, were content.

By the time I had returned from working on the play in Massachusetts, Emma and Evil had already established sleeping arrangements. At bedtime, I brought the old dog bed upstairs and found Sarge at his usual spot on the rug and Evil on my usual side of the bed.

"No, no, no," I announced to the dog and Emma. "This is not going to happen."

I put down the dog bed and pointed to it. "Here. This is yours." As Evil was still only a puppy, it was easy enough to pick her up and place her on it. By the time I turned back to my bed, she was already shooting through the air, landing on my pillow.

Emma laughed, and I thought it was funny too. The first time, the second, then less amusing past the fourth. By the time we reached the eightieth, Emma joined the training session. She held Evil down on the dog bed while I quickly slipped under the covers. When she let Evil go, we both expected her to rocket onto her side of the bed, but that didn't happen. Instead, Evil watched as Emma settled into her usual sleeping place. We congratulated each other on a job well done, then turned out the lights.

With her impeccable timing, Evil waited until we had both fallen asleep before climbing into bed between us. If she had left it at that, she might have proven she wasn't so much of a disturbance. It was a king-size bed; there was room. But Evil had to be the king.

In my dream I was falling through the sky—a short fall since I landed on the bedroom floor. With super puppy strength, she had nudged me to the side of the mattress with her four legs, then pressed against me so my inclination was to turn over and away from her.

"What happened?" Emma called out, hearing a thud followed by every swear word I could remember at 2 a.m.

"She kicked me out!"

"How? She's a little puppy."

Evil patiently awaited my counter strike. "You're out!" I said as I grabbed her up and carried her down the stairs to the living room. "You did this to yourself."

I looked at her with all the severity I could manage and pointed to the floor. "Stay! You will sleep here!"

It was so early in our relationship that I was convinced this was checkmate. Emma was sitting up when I returned.

"Is she really staying?" she asked.

"You bet she is," I insisted, glancing quickly over my shoulder. "And we're going to close the door."

"She'll cry."

"So will I unless I get some sleep." I pulled open the drawer in my bedside table. "And I have a secret weapon." Proudly, I showed Emma the small plastic packet containing earplugs that I had brought home from my last flight. "Would you like one? We could both sleep on our other ear."

"Thanks, but I'll get some cotton if I need it," Emma said.

"*When* you need it, you mean." The house was suspiciously quiet except for Sarge's occasional snore.

"I can't believe you did it," Emma said. "I thought she'd come running up after you."

"It's all in the voice," I gassed on. "She might not understand the words, but she hears the tone and knows I mean business."

We had only fallen asleep for a few minutes when we heard the first howl. Not the whiny yips of a puppy, but the howl of a lion who knew food was on the other side of the door. Even more impressive was the frequency Evil found to pierce through even earplugs.

"No matter what," I told Emma as we both stared at the door, "we have to ignore her."

What seemed to be an eternity later, the dog stopped, and the silence was now as ominous as the howling. Still, it didn't take long before we found sleep again.

THUD.

Not a small "thud," but one with the power of a kick by the Green Giant.

THUD.

This time Sarge woke, looking from the door to us, confused.

THUD.

"How can a little dog be so loud?" Emma wondered.

"Maybe she learned to hold a hammer."

THUD.

"This is like a horror movie," Emma said. And how right she was proven to be.

"I have to let her in, or she'll hurt herself."

"Give her a few more slams," I urged. "Maybe she'll knock herself unconscious."

Whether Emma heard me or not, she was already out of the bed and opening the door. Sitting, Evil looked up at her meekly.

"I have an idea, just for tonight," I announced. "Get back into bed and we'll sleep back to back. She can't push both of us off, and if we tuck in the covers, she can't get under them, either."

"Worth a try," Emma agreed. As we got into sleep position, Evil watched us from the open door and Sarge, now standing, shook himself, which was his way of shaking his head. He left us to find a quiet bedroom.

Lights out, and we waited. Was Evil at the base of the bed or on either side? Underneath, prepared to strike when our feet touched the floor? We sorted through possibilities as the fluorescent numbers on the alarm kept changing. Finally, thankfully, slumber.

Sometime later, I woke, surprised. Something hairy had touched my feet. I threw back the covers to see that Evil had submarined under the covers from the foot of the bed and stretched out for the night.

Evil was asleep. Emma and I just stared. "I'll take her downstairs again," I half-heartedly offered.

"I'll do it," Emma said.

Exhausted and sleep deprived, neither of us moved.

"We can't let her get away with this," I insisted. "This is the kind of behavior that leads to delinquency. Let a little thing go like stealing change from the bureau, then a candy bar from a store, and before you know it, they're working on Wall Street."

"Remember to tell Evie that tomorrow," Emma suggested, pulling the covers back up on her.

I turned back to Evil, who hadn't moved. *Or had she?* I found out later that dogs have not one or two but three eyelids. The third, or the nicitans membrane, protects the dog's eye under the first two. If, during sleep, the two outer eyelids are open and the membrane is in sight, it appears that the dog's eyes have turned white or rolled back in their head. And Evil had plenty of eyelids with which to wink.

"In vain the black dog follows you
and hangs close to your flying skirts with hungry fangs."
Horace

CHAPTER FIVE

TRAVELS WITH EVIL

"Let's board the dogs," Emma suggested.

"For six weeks?" I objected. "I don't want Sarge in a kennel for six weeks. We'll take him with us."

"Then we have to take Evie. You know that."

"Not necessarily," I countered. "Maybe a kennel would be good for her. Maybe she'd appreciate us more when we came home."

"She appreciates me already. So we're talking about you again."

I had another card to play. "If we take Evie, we have to take Charlie. And you have to promise not to 'accidentally' open a window and his cage door at the same time."

"Or I can just stay home," Emma argued.

"Why would you do that?"

"You'll be at the theater in rehearsals. Or you'll be in a room all day writing with the door closed," she replied.

"Only because Evil would keep barging in to distract me."

"Evie? Charlie makes noises all day! He imitates you, the dogs, and the kids. That doesn't bother you."

"Charlie wouldn't chew up my computer if I turned my back. She would."

"No, he'd just bite the keys off your keyboard and toss them around the room. How many times has Charlie done that?"

"Charlie was just playing."

"Evie isn't?"

"No. She's as 'playful' as a pack of feral pigs."

Emma stared at me. "You really believe it's personal, don't you?"

"It is personal! She doesn't like me. Every day she proves it. Why can't you see that?"

"You have no patience with her! You do with Sarge and Charlie. Can't *you* see that? Evie's still a puppy! This is your problem! She's not your arch enemy, she's our dog!"

"Your dog," I corrected her.

Emma hesitated. "Is that your real problem?" she asked. With a menagerie to transport, we decided not to fly to Sarasota. Instead, we would drive, and rather than putting the mileage on our aging Toyota, we rented a small van. Even doing that, we estimated it would be less expensive than putting all of us on a plane.

Before leaving, we went about Evil-proofing the new Chevy Express. Thick mats were stretched across the back seat. Metal grating was installed behind the front seats to be certain Evil wouldn't leap into the driver's seat, grab the wheel in her teeth, and drive. Though I kept it to myself, I didn't doubt that Evil would steer us off a cliff or into oncoming traffic. Adding insult to injury, I was certain she'd be the only survivor.

Sarge hopped into the back seat and immediately went to sleep. I was never certain if he were playing possum so that Evil would leave him alone, but Sarge seemed to sleep an awful lot whenever she appeared. That or look at me with big, mournful eyes, asking what he had done to deserve such torment at this stage of his life.

After hurling herself at the grating for a stretch, Evil decided it was a battle she couldn't win. Instead, she surprised us by settling down and stretching out long enough to displace Sarge, who meekly retired to the seat behind her.

Every few minutes Emma turned in her seat to observe her dog. With the grate, full view was impossible, but it appeared she was serenely resting. I checked the rear view mirror often, confirming her reports. Our worrying was unnecessary, Emma said, even unfair.

"There are no bad dogs," she insisted. "Only bad owners. You always expect the worst from her. She's living down to your expectations."

She said more, but it didn't register. I was already bracing myself for Evil's sneak attack. Was she currently wetting through the mats? Chewing through the seat belts? No, they were under the mats; how could she reach them?

"Let's pull into the next rest stop," I suggested. "We can let the dogs out and give them some water."

Emma was surprised at my concern. We had driven only a little over an hour; a stop seemed premature. Still, she agreed, and we turned into the exit, following the directional signs to the parking lot.

Sliding the van door open, I had Evil's leash in hand, attaching it swiftly to her collar before she could launch her escape. Instead, she stepped down calmly and I saw the hand-iwork she had concealed. Evil had chewed through the heavy mats and beyond, chomping through the leather cushions to the springs.

I looked from the seat slaughter to Evil, now sitting in a placid pose on the blacktop beside me. Emma swore her expression was one of shame. I saw no shame, only satisfaction. Evil's march through Florida had begun.

That night we each took turns walking the dogs around the grounds of the Stay Awhile hotel while the other tried to safe-ty-proof our room. Our bags were hidden in the closet. One of the bags had been seriously attacked at home. Packing, both of us had our open suitcases on the bed. Sitting down for a quick lunch, our small talk was interrupted by Evil coming proudly down the stairs with my new jeans clamped between her teeth.

She wouldn't release them, forcing a tug of war that only stopped with the sound of a rip. Needless to say, when we went back upstairs, all my packed clothes were scattered around the room, while Emma's suitcase was untouched.

I put anything in the hotel room that looked chewable onto the highest shelf in the closet, closed its door, and opened the bedside table drawer to remove the Gideon Bible. Even con-cealed there, I had no doubt Gideon was in danger. Evil would sense its presence and be on that Bible like a hawk on a rabbit. I slid it deep under the mattress. Charlie commented with the sound effect of a flush.

Emma returned with the dogs. She and Sarge were clearly bushed. Evil scanned the room, sensing change.

"I have an idea," Emma said. "Let's go downstairs to the lounge, order something to eat, and have drinks while we wait. We'll be back in a half-hour max. The dogs will be fine." I was less confident. "In half an hour she might learn to use the phone and have us arrested for abandonment."

Emma didn't agree but took it seriously enough to offer another suggestion. The bathroom was large and its floor tiled. The sink and toilet were porcelain and couldn't be destroyed unless Evil found a jackhammer. If we put Evil in there for the short time we'd be gone with water, food, and a toy, even Emma saw no possibility of annihilation.

I looked at Evil, suspecting she understood every word. Still, I agreed. Having time away from Evil was a risk worth taking. She followed her bowls and toy into the bathroom and was sitting in a demure normal dog pose when we closed the door behind us. We listened. Silence. Waited for a minute—still not a sound.

Sarge was already snoring on the bed, relieved that for now, at least, he didn't have to watch his back. Charlie called to us from his cage as we left the room.

"See you later!" Was his squawk following it a cackle?

Over drinks at the hotel bar, Emma and I played Rock Paper Scissors to determine which of us would call the car rental company to report the damage. I lost, but even that didn't affect the calm that was descending now that the day's driving was done.

"Do you remember the days when we didn't go to hotels to sleep?" I asked.

For the first time that day, we both laughed. Shared memories led to another round of drinks, Emma's gin and tonic and my Coors Light. She was in such a good mood that she didn't call me out for being a lightweight drinker. Usually, after I ordered Coors Light, I was prepared for a comment like, "Next time try water, it's cheaper."

I took Emma's hand and leaned toward her and suggested in my best seductive whisper: "What do you think of leaving Evie in the bathroom for a while when we get back to the room?" Unlike Sarge, Evil had an instinct that told her when we were using the bed for anything but slumber. She would stand outside the closed door barking or, when that didn't work, whining pitifully. My solution was earplugs; Emma's was to get more and more distracted until she got up and opened the door. Like a heat-seeking missile, Evil would launch herself through the door and onto our bed.

Caninus interruptus.

"What if she does her usual crying?" Emma wanted to know.

"There's a clock radio, isn't there? Every hotel has one. We put on whatever comes in clearest and crank up the volume." The station didn't matter. By now, I could get amorous listening to NPR.

We approached our door slowly, bracing ourselves for the barking we were sure to hear. But there was none. Surprised, we exchanged smiles.

I put the key in the door and opened it.

Evil greeted us, wagging her tail. Sarge was now pressed muzzle first into a corner of the room, pretending to be anywhere else.

"Hola!" Charlie called.

"But how could she—?" Emma began.

My roar of disbelief stopped her. She joined me at the bathroom door, still closed but bearing a large, ragged hole where Evil had chewed through the wood to escape. Emma went to Evil while I stared, incredulous. *How did she do it?* How did she manage to get a bite hold on a solid wooden door? How, in that short a time, had she crunched through almost two inches of oak?

"Calm down," Emma told me, on her knees petting Evil. "She must have done it because she was terrified."

"*I'm* terrified!"

Evil met my eyes without flinching.

"You're ridiculous," Emma told me. "She's still a puppy. Puppies chew. It was our fault to leave her alone. We won't do it again."

I winced at the thought of being handcuffed to Evil for the rest of my days.

"We'll just pay for the door. It will be fine," Emma continued. "How much could it be?"

We found our answer when we were handed a bill at checkout the next morning.

From Raleigh all the way to Sarasota, no one spoke, barked, or whimpered.

"Can we put it behind us?" Emma finally asked. "It's over."

Not really. It wasn't over until we paid the three-hundred-dollar bill for the hotel door with two hundred more added for labor.

We had taken additional insurance out on the rental van but were told it was for accidents, and no matter how hard I tried, I couldn't convince the company that chewing through the back seat was an accident.

Our own insurance agent told me the same, after he stopped laughing.

All bills combined, Emma and I could have flown first class to the Caribbean for a month and paid a pet sitter to stay with Evil, Sarge, and Charlie back home. *But would the pet sitter have survived?*

Emma had no interest in hearing this. We had resumed our road trip with some changes to the car arrangements. The grill was now down. It had blocked us from total view of Evil and, this time, we were determined to keep our eyes on her every move. To prevent her from hurtling into the front seat, we hooked a safety belt around the halter we'd bought to encircle her.

"Let's just own it and move on. We made some bad choices. Neither of us have ever raised a dog from a puppy," Emma finally said.

And one of us never would have tried, I thought, but opted for diplomacy.

"True enough," I agreed. "But there's nature and there's nurture. What if Evil's behavior isn't just a matter of our incompetent 'nurturing' but her 'nature' itself? If Caesar Milan had been Ted Bundy's big brother, would Ted have been better behaved?"

Emma sighed and turned up the radio, an oldies station. You know you're getting older when most "oldies" are from the first records you ever bought.

I glanced in the rear view mirror.

There are pet owners who swear their dog smiles. I have read some experts who regard that expression as a "smile of submission." "Submissive" is a word that could never be used to describe Evil. Her grin was a taunt of triumph, a promise of worse to come.

"Rolling Stones next," the radio DJ declared. *"Sympathy for the Devil!"*

"Breed not a savage dog or permit a loose stairway."
The Talmud

CHAPTER SIX

EVIL IN PARADISE

Sarasota is a beautiful city, the cultural heart of Florida. Richard Hopkins, Artistic Director of the Florida Studio Theater, which had done several shows of mine, was kind enough to put me "in residence" there. In return for this escape from winter, I taught a playwrighting class, comprised mostly of people who had retired from successful careers and now wanted to tell their stories.

Emma, the menagerie, and I were housed on one floor of a building that could have been mistaken for college fraternity housing. It was perfect for our situation. Furniture and décor were rudimentary. Nothing valuable that could be chewed; nothing so precious it couldn't survive being bumped to the floor.

Nevertheless, we were determined to cover every couch with sheets, and then piled pots and pans on top to keep both dogs off them. Sarge quickly resigned himself to sleeping on the rug at our bedside. Evil, thwarted, roamed, restless with resentment, through the apartment, casing each room.

The rooms had air conditioning, but with the mild temperature, we preferred to open the windows so breezes could cool the house. There were easily two dozen screens on the house's windows as well as a screened-in porch.

Once we settled in, I tried to leave the house as stealthily as possible to run some errands. Evil was lying in wait to jump me once my hand touched the back doorknob. Her paws pressed heavily on my back, I turned to face her, tearing two strips down my T-shirt as I did. Emma appeared, hearing me vent.

"Look at my shirt! What are we going to do with this dog?"

She slowly nodded. "It looks like you'd better take her to get her nails clipped."

There were two possible responses here. The first was to remind Emma that Evil was her dog, and it wasn't her torn shirt. The second, if I wanted to sleep in the bed and not on the couch piled with kitchen utensils, was to disregard response one.

Without a word, I closed the screen door, leaving Emma and Evil, the two amigas, behind me.

There was a reason I tried to leave the house unnoticed. Like all dogs, Evil loved to ride in the car. Most dogs get their kicks by sticking their head out of a car window to feel the rush of a 65-miles-per-hour breeze. Admittedly, it's not my idea of fun, but there's some understandable wind-in-your-hair sense of adventure to it. Evil, instead, claws her way to the console between the driver and passenger seats, then leaps forward so that her two front legs are on the dashboard and her head pushed as close to the glass as possible. To someone looking in from the outside, Evil would appear to be a slightly crushed bobble head wedged between windshield and dash.

This makes driving a challenge. Almost always it necessitates pulling over, pushing her into the back seat, and then gripping onto the headrest on the passenger's seat with my right arm to form a wall she can't get through.

It was a small consolation, I thought, getting into the rental van Evil had already been at war with, that I would be driving alone. She was secured in the apartment.

I turned the key, and the motor came to life as I put the van into reverse. As I rolled back over the driveway stones, I heard Emma shouting, "No, Evie!" Then I watched as Evil leapt through the living room screen as easily as punching through tissue paper. For a moment she seemed suspended in the air before dropping five feet to the garden below.

She raced to the van, bounded up to my driver's window, and stared at me expectantly. Pretending I didn't see her, I resumed, slowly backing out of the driveway and staring straight ahead. Evil kept pace. Should I gun it and take the chance she'd run after me? This promised possibilities. If she ran after me, could I find a nearby highway and see if she could hold on at seventy-five miles an hour while dodging Florida's senior drivers?

But Emma was still watching from the house. Her arms folded across her chest indicated that any displeasure with Evil had shifted to a watchfulness at my next move.

I stopped. If I got out to open the back door for her to hop in, it would lead to Evil racing around the vehicle, daring me to catch her. Instead, I opened the back windows, reversed a few inches, and Evil leaped up through one and into the van.

Emma smiled. I waved. Evil, contented, sat happily in the back seat. The moment we were out of sight, Evil rocketed into her usual position, balanced on the console, nose pressing against the windshield, her front feet blocking my gearshift.

Evil had won again. I didn't keep score; there was no point. So far, I had never even made it onto the scoreboard.

By now, I'm sure some of you are getting frustrated, certain you already know a simple solution to solving the problem of Evil.

"Crate training!" you'd tell me. "If you had just brought her up by having her sleep in a crate every night, she'd have boundaries and think of it as her home! If you had to leave her alone, you could toss in a toy, some food, some water, and she'd stay there, safe and happy. And you'd be, too!"

Simple enough, yes. But Evil is not simple.

"Be a corporal act of mercy
if someone would take the life of that bloody dog."
James Joyce, *Ulysses*

CHAPTER SEVEN

EVIL AND HOUDINI

Harry Houdini and his wife, Bess, were great dog lovers. Not much about their pets has survived history, but the little we do know of Charles and Bobby became fascinating to me soon after the arrival of Evil.

Charles, the Houdini's Pomeranian, came from royalty. The Grand Duke of Russia presented the couple with this small ball of white fur in 1903. While touring Europe, according to Kenneth Silverman in his book *HOUDINI!!!!: The Career of Ehrich Weiss*, several countries refused to have animals brought through their borders. Houdini thwarted this embargo "using one of Ching Ling Foo's conjuring methods," and Charles continued traveling with his adoptive parents.

Houdini and Bess were heartbroken when Charles died in 1909. Before long, they took Bobby, of unknown lineage, into the fold. Silverman reports that Houdini taught their new dog how to escape from both a pair of miniature handcuffs and a straitjacket. Proudly, Houdini put him into the act as "Bobby the Handcuff King."

It was Bobby, I think, who was a role model for Evil. I'm not claiming Evil read Silverman's book, but I can attest to her chewing it into soggy pieces before I finished reading it. Could Evil have absorbed Bobby's talents for escape by ingesting them?

As you might expect, after Evil's escape from the hotel bathroom by gnawing through its solid wooden door, she scoffed at any further attempts to restrain her. From that point on, Evil became the roadrunner to my coyote. I was determined this canine breakout queen would not prevail a second time. Or a third time. Or a fourth. In retrospect, it forced me to face the fact that Evil had powers Houdini would envy.

By then, Evil had grown to a formidable forty-two pounds. Her favorite method of attack was disguised as a warmhearted welcome. The moment you left her company, even by going briefly into another room, you returned to her launching herself to greet you, front paws slamming down on your shoulders, causing you to step back, lose balance, and fall backwards to the ground. Even if you were able to keep your balance, she made sure her face was close enough to yours that you were unable to ignore her breath and the triumph in her eyes. Panting in victory, she didn't need words to convey her message: "You fell for it again! Now, go fetch me a treat, Biscuit Boy!"

I bought a large black steel cage that would fold up for traveling and snap quickly into shape as a pen after arrival. Laying out cage sections and hardware across my office floor, I ignored Evil watching me and carefully followed all assembly instructions, paying particular attention to the bolt feature that securely locked it.

The bolt caught Evil's eye as well. She came closer, sniffed it, and, unimpressed, left the room with a blithe step.

I was eager to test my cage against her wits. A short time later, I put a bowl of water inside its bars and enticed Evil into it with a rawhide bone, which I left for her. I convinced Emma that it was the perfect day to take a walk around the neighborhood and that the downpour would be good for our complexions.

"Why are we walking in the rain and the animals are back in the dry house?" Emma asked as I angled to get more protection under her umbrella.

"I want to make sure the cage works."

"Okay. So?"

"Evil's not going to try to get out if we're there." "Evie. And why is that a bad thing?"

"Because we want to be sure the cage will hold her," I explained. "If we were in the house now, she wouldn't even try to break out because she might reveal her escape secrets. If she's still in the cage when we get back, then we know it works."

We had taken our third walk around the block when Emma insisted on going home because the lightning strikes were hitting closer.

On the front porch, both of us held our breath. *Would Evil be there to greet us, as she had been in the Florida hotel, flaunting her freedom?*

I opened the door and we looked into the foyer.

No Evil.

Relieved, we walked slowly through the house, stopping at my office. Spread out on the floor were pieces of the once-assembled cage, a few still mutually attached, others bent and flung across the room.

We looked at each other, incredulous. At that moment Evil entered from behind us and leaned contentedly against Emma's leg.

"How?" I asked.

"You must have made some mistake assembling it," Emma asserted.

Evil looked up at her, waving her tail to confirm it. I picked up the side of the cage the door was built into. It was still bolted.

"I didn't make a mistake," I insisted. "And she didn't get out through the cage door. How did she do it, then? How did she take it apart from the inside?"

Emma shrugged. "If you can't figure that out, you should return it and get a stronger cage." She went into the kitchen to start dinner, Evil following, wagging her tail to a new beat.

No. This cage was strong. The metal bars were thick and all the connections solid. There was no reason this cage shouldn't have held Evil and no way I was going to let her win. Pride. We know what follows it. Instead of looking ahead, dreaming of victory, I should have looked to the past and learned from history. Particularly my experience with Evil's Great Escape. She had broken out of our enclosed property without even the use of a motorcycle.

For several years, our fenced-in backyard had given Sarge a huge space within which to play. Sarge could run, should he ever decide to, or roam at his own pace, ignoring all balls and sticks thrown for him to fetch, and, instead, stretch out in the sun, peacefully observing the squirrels scuttling past and over him. Until the arrival of Evil, Sarge had had an easygoing "live and let live" disposition. After that, Sarge's credo was modified to "live and leave me alone."

Never once had Sarge escaped. I doubt he'd ever entertained the idea. What could be on the other side of the fence that he didn't have here? Two meals a day he didn't have to hunt down or dig through trash to find, frequent treats, a soft dog bed, and continual pats and kind words. He might not understand what we said, but he liked the way we said it.

After ingesting my Houdini book, Evil looked at the backyard as a challenge. Escaping not only proved her intelligence but certified my idiocy, believing I could stop her.

She also relished public shaming. After we noticed Evil's breakout and long patrolled the neighborhood for a sight of her, our search would end with an irritated call from a stranger, wondering why we let our poor dog roam free. Evil would conclude her wanderings by finding someone doing yard work or getting out of their car and approaching them, head down, too dejected to wag her tail.

"Are you lost, girl?"

A few piteous dog whimpers and Evil's patsy would rush to the phone and call her uncaring owners, who shouldn't be allowed to have a dog at all. After Evil's first disappearance, I inspected every foot of fencing, fortifying its base with bricks and rocks to make certain escape wasn't a possibility.

After her second flight I nailed down tent spikes that held the fencing close to the ground to eliminate any chance of going under it.

After Evil's third escape I considered land mines but gave up on that idea while Emma got angry at what she thought was my joking.

But the difference between a yard and a cage is thousands of feet to safeguard. The cage can be secured, every inch of it fortified as the walls of Alcatraz. No, not Alcatraz; people escaped from there. More like Gilligan's Island, where the castaways never escaped, despite the professor's ability to build a nuclear reactor but not a raft.

I went to the hardware store and bought two dozen tiny clamps. I would make Evil's cage impossible to dissemble with teeth, claws, or anything less than a blowtorch.

I fortified every joint of the cage, securing each panel. Seeing Evil observing me, I smiled.

"Dare you," I challenged her.

My confidence should have been shaken when Evil walked into the cage without being lured by water, food, or toy. She looked back at me as if to invite me to join her. But I was wary. I knew that if Emma locked me in the cage, I would be in there until the time came when she decided to let me out. For that reason, I kept out of it, fortifying security only from the outside.

Closing the door on Evil, I sought out Emma. She was in her office on the second floor, finishing up a call with a colleague on her counseling team. Noticing me in her doorway, she gave me a signal to wait and concluded her conversation.

"I've got a visitor, Jackie. Got to go. He pouts when he's kept waiting."

She hung up and waited to hear the reason I needed her attention.

"Your dog is locked up for life," I said with considerable pride. "She's not getting out until we free her."

"You put her in that cage again?"

"I did, and I'm telling you now that we're not knocking off time for good behavior." Emma laughed. I found myself flushed with gratitude. I hadn't heard that laugh for a very long time.

I walked toward her, wanting to pull her up into an embrace, but I didn't have that chance. Evil had beaten me to it. Emma turned away and hugged the dog, who stood on two legs behind her.

Was I hallucinating? Without saying another word, I ran down to the living room. The cage's gate was closed and locked. Its walls, ceiling, and floor intact.

And it was empty.

Emma and Evil had followed me down. Emma saw my despair, while Evil relished it.

"This is physically impossible," I managed.

"It isn't," Emma soothed me. "It's possible because you were so proud of securing it, you didn't pay enough attention to the door bolt. Evie must have shaken it loose."

"But it's locked now!"

"It probably fell back into place after she got out."

"I tested the bolt. It was definitely secure."

"You're positive. Completely, without a doubt, positive?"

"Yes! Definitely! I *think* …'

"Mark, you did your best. You're tired. Let's go to bed and read. You can try again tomorrow." Emma kissed me on the cheek.

We went upstairs and settled in, Evil, as usual, between us. Emma picked up the book on her nightstand, the latest non-fiction serial killer bestseller. I opted for fiction and returned to a novel by Tony Hillerman in his series featuring Navajo homicide detective Joe Leaphorn and his sergeant, Jim Chee. I prefer my murders to be fictional. After a few chapters, I closed the book to put it on the bedside table when I realized I wasn't just staring at the book's cover but the clue to Evil's escape.

"Emma! Look!" She was sleeping heavily by the sound of it, but this was too important to wait.

"Mhhh?"

I held the book in front of her for her to see.

"Wha …?"

"Read the title!"

"The Shapeshifter."

"Yes! A shapeshifter is a Navajo witch. It can take on different forms, human or animal."

"That's nice. Goodnight."

"It explains Evil!"

"Evie! And keep your voice down, you'll wake her!"

Evil, the barrier between us, hadn't moved a muscle.

Excited, I pressed on. Shapeshifters could be found throughout history. In Greek mythology, the god Narcissus transformed himself into a flower. Dracula became a bat; J. K. Rowling's Remis Lupin could change into a werewolf, as could the Twilight Saga's shapeshifters of the Quileute tribe.

"Those are all imaginary characters," Emma said, growing more irritated as she woke.

"But there are real animals who can do the same. They compress themselves! Mice and rats can squeeze through the tiniest opening. Same thing for an octopus! They escape their tanks all the time!"

"So maybe Evie transformed into an octopus, slid through your cage bars, then turned herself back into a dog." Emma didn't give me a chance to respond, which was probably a good thing. "Go to sleep. I'm going to pretend you had a terrible dream, so terrible you were insensitive enough to wake me, babbling nonsense."

"Emma ..."

"Goodnight! We'll talk about it in the morning. If we're talking."

She turned her back to me and was instantly asleep.

Only then did Evil, playing possum, raise her head to look at me. I stared back, refusing to blink. Evil met the challenge. For what seemed like an eternity, our eyes were locked, until she gave out with a brief bark.

Emma bolted up. "Mark! Stop playing with the dog! I need to sleep!"

She turned on her side and Evil, satisfied, closed her eyes to dream of romping in Hades.

Whether because of frustration or desperation, I knew I'd be awake thinking all night. I'd been sure from the start that this animal was much more than a dog. It was time to discover what she really was.

I'll need help, I decided. *Serious help. It's time to journey into the belly of the beast.*

"I fled him down the nights and down the days."
Francis Thompson, "*The Hound of Heaven*"

CHAPTER EIGHT

TRAINING EVIL

Over time, and excepting her romp at World O' Pups, Evil went through three trainers. While we were in Sarasota, we found the first trainer from her ad in the local newspaper. "There is no dog who can't be trained," Emma read. I was more impressed by the trainer's next claim: "Money back guarantee."

FLORENCE: Florence was a middle-aged woman with orange-red hair who appeared, wearing a matching brown shirt, shorts, and knee socks. All that was missing was a pith helmet.

I had taken Sarge out to the backyard, where he could play and not have to witness whatever humiliations Evil might put Florence through. I let the trainer in while Emma held tight to Evil's collar, preventing her usual greeting of guests, which included jumping up to put her paws on their shoulders, make full body contact, and do as much face licking as possible before the visitor's escape reflex kicked in.

Once calmed, Evil allowed Florence to pet her as she asked us, "What behaviors need modification?"

"She pretty much mugs anyone coming into the house," I began. "She's not a huge dog, but it's all muscle. You don't walk her, she walks you. Drags you if she's in a hurry. She understands words like 'dinner and 'dog park' but plays stupid with things like 'no' or 'get the hell off me.'"

"She's a good dog," Emma cut in, assuming the role of defense attorney. "I have more success with her than Mark does, but whatever we try to teach her is a struggle."

"With Emma it's a struggle. With me it's a war," I couldn't help but add.

"You're a beautiful dog, aren't you, Evie?" Florence cooed. "Look what I have for you." She reached into her large carpetbag. "My secret weapon." She pulled out a Ziploc bag containing pigs in blankets. "I cut each one in half, since we don't want to overfeed her, but dogs love them."

So did I. If she popped a few in the microwave, I'd be happy to roll over and play dead.

"She's house trained, of course," Emma continued. "She was in an obedience class as a puppy, but nothing else much stuck."

"Especially the obedience," I added.

"Let's start with something basic," Florence suggested. "You say she jumps on people to greet them. She does that because she's excited. Evie wants to get close and make sure you see her. To change that, you have to take away what she wants: eye-to-eye contact. When she jumps up, you simply turn your back on her. If she comes to your front, you turn again. You keep this up every time she greets you. Trust me, she'll learn not to. When she gives up jumping, you praise her—'Good dog! Good dog!'—and reward her with a treat. Gradually, she won't need the treat, just the praise."

Everything Florence said was logical if you were training a dog. But training Evil?

Florence told us she would go outside and, after a few minutes, ring the doorbell. Class would begin.

Emma and I sat in the living room. I tossed Evil the latest indestructible dog toy for her to destroy. She just sniffed and walked away, not interested. Emma was surprised she didn't want to chew on it. I wasn't.

"She's not interested in chewing, she's interested in carnage. Look at her pounce on any stuffed animal we give her. First she takes it and shakes it as hard and fast as she can. If it were a squirrel, it would have its back and neck broken. Then she drops it and guts it in seconds. Forget hard rubber toys. Where's the fun there? Fun to her is sadism to us."

The doorbell cut off any reply Emma would have made. Evil followed her to the door, and when Emma opened it, leaped past her toward Florence, already turning her back.

Evil hit her hard. If I knew football, I would compare her to the NFL's most powerful tackler. She lifted Florence off her feet, and the trainer came down, fortunately on grass and not sidewalk. We rushed to her and helped her up as she insisted nothing was broken.

"She's a strong girl," Florence managed with the breath she had left.

Evil, meanwhile, who had her head in the trainer's carpetbag, gulped them down, plastic bag included.

"Bad dog, Evie!" Florence shouted, advancing on her. "Bad, bad dog!"

Evil's response was to tear off down the street with a greyhound's speed.

From the house we heard Charlie's imitation of me laughing.

"It's our fault. We didn't put her leash on!" Emma said.

"We didn't expect her to do a hit and run," I offered.

Florence announced that the training session was over, asked to be paid in cash, and said she had to check her calendar before committing to another training date. As you've probably already guessed, we never saw her, or our cash, again.

For us, the fun was just beginning. After letting Sarge into the house and getting a leash, we went from training Evil to tracking her. When Emma got into the van with me, I couldn't help but think she suspected that, left alone, I'd simply drive around the corner and just park.

"She's got a sense of direction. She'll come back," I said as we pulled out. "Lassie always came home."

"She doesn't know this city like she knows our town." I decided to enjoy the ride. Driving was the easy part.

Capturing Evil, once we spotted her, was the challenge. After about twenty minutes, we spotted her. She was on the front lawn with a small family that had turned into her fan club. Mother, father, and their toddler daughter petted Evil and cooed over what a beautiful dog she was. Evil was wagging her tail but stopped when she spotted us in the van.

"She'll run away from me," I told Emma. "Why don't you try?"

"Evie!" Emma called, getting out of the car. "Look what I have for you!"

"Treats!" Evil ran to meet her as Emma waved to the family. Taking the treat from her hand, she bolted before Emma could clip on her leash.

"It begins," I sighed.

Nearly a half hour of Evil playing fake out rope-a-dope with Emma and Evil's entourage Fan Club Family began. Someone would slowly approach Evil, talking soothingly as they did so, and a millisecond before they could grab hold of the dog's collar, she would race away. Evil would stop at a distance, temptingly close, look back at her audience, and wait for the fun to resume.

By now, Evil was about three blocks away from where we had found her.

I had followed in the car, which I noticed Evil was tracking, occasionally glancing over her shoulder. By now, I was starving for dinner, having missed lunch. Not for the first time, hunger was the mother of invention.

"Emma!" I called. "Come here! I have an idea!" When Emma approached the car, I told her to get in.

"We are not leaving her!" she insisted.

"But what if she thought we were?"

Emma sparked to the idea and climbed into the passenger seat. Evil watched as I pulled from the curb and headed down the street. "She's running after us!" Emma reported, her voice filled with joyful relief.

By now, Evil was keeping pace with the car, seemingly intent on proving she could outrace it, but when I slowed to a stop, she retreated once again.

"Now what?" Emma wondered.

"We step up our game." I told her my idea and she just looked at me.

"Really?"

"Come on," I said. "Like we can do any worse than we're doing now?"

Emma got into the back seat and I started the car again. Evil waited until we had driven a hundred feet, then loped off after us. I stepped on the gas.

"Mark! Slow down!" Emma shouted. I didn't.

Evil was abreast of the car, now running at maximum speed to catch up. Once she was abreast of us, I called back to Emma, "Now!"

Emma slid back the passenger door. Surprised but not breaking stride, Evil looked in to see Emma turn away from her. Whether prompted by the lesson and feeling snubbed or simply tired of the game, Evil leaped into the car and Emma shut the door after her.

Evil licked Emma's face as she hugged and fussed over her, then returned to the front seat.

"Good idea," Emma admitted.

"Can I lick your face when we get home?"

She leaned over and kissed me. "I do love you, you know."

I told her I did, then wondered the rest of the drive why it sounded like Emma was convincing herself, not me.

MOONROCK: Back in Woodstock, enough time had passed that we convinced ourselves that, with the right person, Evil could be trained. Moonrock Dietz, the man who cut our grass, was a lifelong Woodstock resident. Since moving here a few years back, I'd gradually become aware of the town's caste system. "Real" Woodstockers were those whose families had lived here long before the 1969 rock festival, "An Aquarian Exposition: 3 Days of Peace and Music," which was not held in Woodstock at all but in Bethel, forty miles southwest.

Old timey Woodstock residents were no fans of counterculture, first proven years before when the town snubbed the artists and creative types moving to the area to the point of refusing to bury them in the same cemetery as normal folk. In 1934, the artists established their own burial ground. Present residents include artist Milton Avery; musicians Levon Helm, Rick Danko, and John Herald; and Howard Koch, one of *Casablanca*'s three screenwriters.

Naturally, Woodstock's townies hated the hippies who subsequently settled in their burg, making them feel equally unwelcome. In recent years, as property prices soared with the purchases of wealthy weekenders fleeing New York City, townies and hippies found they had one thing in common: They hated the preppies and millionaires.

Moonrock's parents swear they attended the Woodstock Festival, a claim made by millions of rock fans despite the fact there were "only" 400,000 attendees.

Still, I believe Moonrock's parents on the strength of their son's name alone. Moonrock was a gentle man who loved animals. Sarge was always happy to see him, and Evil even more so. She followed him around the yard and Moonrock talked to her, the gist of which was drowned out by the lawn mower's motor.

"Do you see how well she gets along with him?" Emma asked as we watched them through the kitchen window.

"I do. Do you think he wants a dog?"

"Stop. What I'm saying is that he's not raising his voice, he's just having a nice conversation with her. Maybe you can try that."

"I'll try anything," I said. "Do I have to mow the lawn while we talk?"

Not answering, Emma went out the kitchen door into the backyard and signaled to Moonrock. Through the window screen I could hear Emma telling him of Evil's lack of interest in being trained. He looked down at her as Emma asked if he ever worked with dogs.

"Oh, yeah! I trained mine from a puppy, and my neighbor's too. Dogs are awesome!"

"Do you think you could train Evie?"

Moonrock went down on one knee before the dog and spoke to her.

"What do you think, girl? Do we want to do this?"

I expected Evil to give him the paw instead of the finger, but she didn't. She barked and wagged her tail. Emma was excited. Moonrock was excited. I was surprised but hopeful. Evil did bond with Moonrock. Whether it was because he trailed the scent of pot was irrelevant. If drugs altered Evil's behavior, I'd be happy to feed her cocaine kibble.

"Can I take her home with me?" Moonrock asked.

"Yes!" I shouted from the house. Emma turned around and mouthed "Watch it!"

"I've got all my crystals there." Moonrock was no longer speaking to Emma but to Evil. "My white quartz stokes up your energy and concentration. And my rose quartz gives good vibes. Peace and harmony to your mind and body. And I got obsidian, which kicks negativity's ass."

Far be it from me to question the crystals of a man named Moonrock.

Evil happily followed him to his van and they were off. Emma was excited that we'd finally found someone who could train her dog in rudimentary behaviors.

I was excited because it was a vacation from Evil. I was hoping Moonrock trained like he cut grass: very slowly. Or maybe one of his crystals wiped out memory and they'd never find their way back.

We were surprised when Moonrock's van pulled into the driveway only two days later. Evil ran to Emma and Moonrock swelled with pride.

"She's trained already?" I asked, doubtful.

"Evie! Sit!" he called out in response.

Evil turned away from Emma and sat, obedient, facing Moonrock.

Needless to say, this seemed more miraculous to us than the Shroud of Turin.

"Good girl!" Moonrock said, scratching the dog's head. "Now, stay!" Evil sat placidly in place, watching him walk to the edge of the fenced-in yard.

"Evie! Come!" he called. Evil raced toward him. "Now, sit!" Moonrock added, and she sat.

Emma turned to me, in shock. I was confused. *Is this a dog double? Did he conk Evil on the head with a hunk of crystal?*

"Evie, lie down. Evie, roll over. Evie, shake hands." Evil did everything requested, even putting her paw in Moonrock's hand.

"Blows your mind, right?" Moonrock said, grinning.

"Wide open. It's amazing," I said.

"Thank you, thank you," Emma added.

"Your turn," Moonrock told us.

"Go ahead, Mark," Emma urged.

I called to Evil, who was staring at me from across the yard.

"Evie! Come!" She sat, not moving a muscle. I turned to Emma. Never again could she say that this dog and I were not locked in a blood feud.

"Evie! Come here, girl!" Emma shouted.

Again, no response. Shocked and embarrassed, Moonrock approached us while Evil remained across the yard.

"I don't get it," Moonrock said, confused. He turned back toward the dog.

"Evie! Come here!"

Evil lay down in the grass and stretched.

"Up, girl!" Moonrock urged the reclining dog. "Evie, roll over!" Evil stood, yawned, and walked past us toward the house.

"What just happened?" Emma asked. We were all bewildered. It was like watching someone run a three-minute mile and then, seconds later, seeing the same runner unable to keep pace with a geezer using a walker.

"You saw her do it, right?" Moonrock asked us. "I mean, it really happened!" He was starting to panic, doubting himself. Had he just trained a dog, or was all this a flashback from another dog he'd trained earlier?

"It happened," I assured him. "She did everything you asked her to do."

"Then why won't she do it now?" Emma had moved past surprise to frustration.

"Rope-a-dope," I said.

"What does that mean?" Emma demanded.

"Fakeout. She proved she could be trained if she wanted to be. But her choice is not to listen to any of us."

"That's cold, man," Moonrock murmured. "Evil," I corrected him. "That's evil."

BUCK: Moonrock's failure lit a fire under Emma. Evil would be trained no matter what the cost. It turned out to be very costly.

"You want Buck Cayman," Judd, the owner of the Ulster Feed Shop, advised us. "The man has the best reputation in this county—probably the state. He's expensive, but you get what you pay for, am I right? Buck has the touch. Could be his background."

"Which is what?" I had to ask.

"Prison guard. Different stories on how that went south, but the fact is, he's damn good with dogs."

Buck Cayman was the first man I'd ever met who chewed tobacco while having a conversation. When he arrived at our door wearing sunglasses, cowboy boots, and yellow, heavy-duty work gloves, I think even Evil was impressed.

Heading out to the backyard with his trainee, he wasted no time. Buck took a collar and a hand held control from his backpack.

"The method's simple," Buck told us as he strapped the bad collar around Evil's neck. "What we got here is an electrified collar. What's this dog's name?"

"Evie," Emma told him.

"Huh. If she listens to me, all's well. If she does not, a low voltage of electricity goes through her collar. If she still doesn't listen, I ratch it up. Good behavior, she gets a treat. Bad behavior, she gets zapped."

I could see the worry on Emma's face.

"Start off easy, something Ava likes to do." Buck took out a rubber ball.

"Ava! Fetch." He threw the ball and Evil watched it bounce to a stop.

"Doesn't she chase balls?"

"Usually. Maybe she's not responding because you got her name wrong. It's Evie, not Ava," Emma told him. From the look Buck gave her, I suddenly felt compassion for every prisoner Buck had ever guarded. He walked to get the ball, then changed his mind and turned back to Evil.

"Ava!" he shouted. "COME HERE!" Nothing. We could see him slowly turn up the amperage of his control. "We're going to level two now. AVA, GET OVER HERE!" He upped the level of electricity, but Evil seemed not to notice. Buck frowned. "Might have a bum collar here."

Removing the collar from Evil and holding it in his hand, he quickly dropped it, stung by the voltage.

"Collar's working," he told us unnecessarily.

Buck went back to his distant spot. "AVA! GET THE HELL OVER HERE! NOW!"

Evil didn't budge.

"Level three," Buck announced, clearly annoyed. "AVA!"

"EVIE," Emma shouted.

"EVA!" Buck repeated. "COME!"

Evil lay down, clearly bored.

"Level four!" said Buck, fingering his control. "EVA! What's wrong with you, dog?"

"Is there a deep fry level?" I asked. After another attempt, then another, Buck's irritation increased with the voltage, as did Emma's concern.

"Don't go higher!" she insisted.

"It's high as she goes already. I've never seen a dog like this! I've trained hundreds, and Ava's in the top one percent of the damnedest dogs I've come across."

Accepting the compliment, Evil walked up to Buck, wagging her tail. "What are you going to do with this dog?" he asked us. Both Buck and I were now staring at Emma.

"I'm going to feed her," Emma said. Evil followed her into the house.

"That's one tough dog. And one tough lady," Buck remarked.

I shrugged. "She loves her."

"We had plenty of that in prison. Women writing inmates, falling in love, even marrying them. It made no sense."

"Nothing you can do, though," I offered.

For the first time, Buck smiled. "You'd be surprised." Later that night, over a game of Scrabble, Emma placed the letters C R A Z E D on the board for double eighteen points and reached into the bag for replacements.

"What do you think about counseling?" she asked.

I was concentrating on using her Z with my I P and her question took me aback.

"Do you feel you need it?" I asked, surprised.

"I think *we* need it."

"We?"

"You. Me. Us. I think we're stuck somewhere. You spend more and more of your time in your office. It's not just to avoid Evie. Even when you're out here in the real world, we don't talk. We watch something on TV or read or play Scrabble."

"We're talking now," I pointed out.

"During a game of Scrabble."

We'd been married thirty-two years. "Isn't it common for couples to feel off-center when their kids have left the house?"

"Maybe," Emma answered. "But it's more than that." *Was she right?*

Emma had once told me that I was good at writing but not good at "life." It's true that she dealt with the real world more than I did. For all our married lives she had served as a buffer so that I could sit alone and make up stories. She organized the children's play dates, coordinated schedules, made sure the car was inspected on time. Every day, I sat behind my desk, losing myself in whatever my current project was. Imagination. Fantasy. Even writing about real life was not real life.

I looked through the floor-to-ceiling windows of the kitchen to see Sarge and Evil lazing on the lawn.

"Don't say it," Emma cautioned.

"Say what?"

"That it's Evie's fault."

I was silent. Emma was annoyed. "What?" she demanded.

"I didn't say it!" I protested.

"You can't blame Evie for everything. We don't talk as much as we used to, and when we do talk, we argue about her."

"We haven't slept alone in our bed for months now," I countered. "This isn't like when the kids were little, and they wanted to be with us. The kids grew out of it. She takes more and more mattress every night. She won't be happy until I'm sleeping next door."

"Can we talk about *us*?" Emma said. "Just the two of us?"

"*Us* has been the three of us."

"You do nothing but try to find fault with her. I think it's easier than finding fault with me."

"It has nothing to do with you," I insisted.

"We just spent our vacation money on a dog trainer for help with Evie's behavior. We have to find someone to help with our own. We need a marriage counselor."

I heard a scratching on the glass door. Evil was signaling to get in. I felt a flush of anger even as I knew I had to swallow it down.

"Leave it to me," I told Emma. "I'll find one."

"Thank you," she said, reaching out for my hand. "I love you."

"And I love you," I said. Emma smiled. "So, can we leave her outside while we finish this game?"

After losing because I lost a turn—who knew "gornish" was not a word?—I went straight to my computer.

Woodstock must be mecca for therapists, psychologists, and psychiatrists, as well as those who feel they can help others through past life and astral communication.

Scrolling down the endless listings on my Macbook Pro, I stopped at one set off by an idyllic picture of a smiling man and woman gazing fondly at their dog strolling between them. "Basic Instincts—Canine Therapy," the ad was titled. "Peace of Mind for You and Your Dog."

Bingo.

"And the dog you take with you will be of no help to you. You can't run away from yourself."
Leo Tolstoy, *Anna Karenina*

CHAPTER NINE

EVIL IN THERAPY

"Mr. St. Germain, I want you to look at her behavior from a dog's point of view. Put yourself in Evie's head," she suggested.

"I'd rather not," I said.

Dr. Leah McShane, Animal Behavior Therapist, had been working with dogs and their owners for thirty-three years. Almost immediately, I knew whose side she took.

I had left Evil behind to avoid her seducing Leah, but clearly it made no difference.

"I read your email describing Evie's behavior," she continued after a brief pause. "I'm curious. What is it you do for a living?"

She scrutinized me with such intensity, I felt like I was being sweated for a murder confession. I found myself putting my hands in my pockets just in case they had blood on them.

"I'm a writer," I told her. "Why?"

"A creative! I understand now." She relaxed. "You make up stories for a living. Exaggerate, sometimes, for the sake of ... entertainment."

"Sometimes," I agreed. "But everything I wrote you about this dog has zero elements of exaggeration. They were factual accounts of Evie's actions."

"You describe your first time meeting Evie as 'hate at first sight.'"

"On her side, yes. Mine took a little longer to work up."

Leah's right eyebrow arched up. I hadn't seen anyone do that since Mr. Spock.

"How old was Evie when your wife brought her home?"

"Ten weeks," I answered, describing how Emma had picked Evie from a litter of puppies. "She climbed over all her brothers and sisters to get to me first," Emma told me proudly.

No surprise there. Trampled siblings.

"So Evie was already settled in your house with your wife and daughter before you came home?" Leah asked.

"That's right."

"You were encroaching on her territory. The first days of a puppy's life can predispose them to certain behaviors. She might have been male averse if she had been roughly handled by a man at the shelter."

"Then wouldn't she respond badly to every male? From what I've seen, she loves every man but me. She practically licks our mailman to death."

"Evie has a primary attachment to your wife because she was the one who rescued her. That forms a strong bond. I've seen dogs who ignore everyone in the family but the person who brought them home."

"I'd love to be ignored! It's the direct opposite of that. She goes out of her way to make my life difficult."

"What if the opposite is true? What if Evie gives you so much attention because she likes you?" she pressed.

"I don't go over to a good friend's house, squat in front of their desk, and empty my bowels."

"Of course not. But your office might appeal to Evie for a number of reasons. She could have left her feces as a gift."

"Then it's the gift that keeps on giving," I told her.

No smile. Another lift of her eyebrow.

"Does your wife have any difficulties with Evie?" "None. Which annoys the hell out of me." What would annoy Emma even more, I didn't mention, was my coming here in the first place. I wouldn't want her, or Evil, to know I was at the point of calling in the cavalry.

"How many dogs have you known that focus on destroying the possessions of only one person in the household?" I pressed. "How many dogs have you treated for chewing through a solid wood door?"

"You shut the door on Evie, confining her to the bathroom. She could be terribly claustrophobic. You could be wearing a deodorant or aftershave that attracts her. To Evie, she's not 'destroying,' she's playing."

I didn't need a weatherman or Bob Dylan to know which way this wind was blowing. Leah wasn't a therapist, she was an apologist. I shouldn't have shown her a picture of Evil. People look at it and see a sweet-tempered, lovable lady pooch and not a Borgia.

So I surrendered. I was done talking. Thanked Leah, and I was at the door before turning back, unable to stop myself.

"What if you're wrong?" I asked her. "What if all your justifications for this dog's behavior are just excuses? Is there any other logical reason she would act this way?"

"There is," Leah conceded. "She hates you."

I was flooded with relief. Of course Evil hated me. I knew that. But to hear someone else confirm it was strangely comforting.

"There is another way to look at it," Leah added. "You believe your wife adopted Evie when your daughter went away to school as a way of replacing her."

"I do."

"Have you considered the possibility that she was replacing you?"

"When a man's dog turns against him, it's time for a wife to pack her trunk and go home to Mama."
Mark Twain

CHAPTER TEN

EVIL AND THE PSYCHIC

"Some have called me clairvoyant, a seer, a mystic. Others just call me wacked."

Esme the extrasensory psychic is known to talk to dead people about the past and the future, and conveys their feelings, and her own, to her clients.

On a gray autumn day, in a coffee house in Ellenville, Esme is addressing an audience gathered to buy her book, *Esme the Extrasensory Psychic*. I was a grudging attendee, pulled along by Emma and my sister, Lynn. They were intrigued by Esme's story and presentation. I kept looking at my watch, hoping we'd be done in time for the nearest happy hour.

Her talk concluded, we stood in line for Esme to sign the books Emma and Lynn had bought.

Emma whispered to me, "Is there any way you can look more skeptical?"

"I can find a mirror and give it a try."

"Why don't you do that? If she has a sixth sense, she'll wallop you with her own book."

"I have a question for her," I said.

"Over your dead body," Emma warned.

Sensing that to be a possibility, my sister pulled me aside. "Go!" she insisted. "You're a wet blanket. Take a walk around the block and I'll ask her your question."

After I made her promise not to tell Emma what it was, I did just that.

Late that night, after Emma had gone to bed with Evil following, I sat in my favorite living room chair to read. I picked up the magazine section of the Sunday paper and saw Emma's copy of *Esme the Extrasensory Psychic* beneath it. Esme of Ellenville stared at me from her cover photo, a septum piercing hanging like a silver sneeze from her nose.

After I'd skimmed the magazine's articles on poisoning our own planet, the death of truth, and a teen star I was fortunate not to be the father of, Esme's book began to look intriguing. I picked it up, intending only to skim it, and finished it at about three in the morning.

I called my sister as early as I dared. I hadn't had the opportunity to be alone with her after yesterday's bookstore event.

"I read Esme the psychic's book," I told her. "Did you ever ask her my question?"

"I did. I felt like a fool, but she didn't blink." "So, what did she say?"

"Yes! She's sensitive to the past lives of animals!"

It was a crisp fall afternoon and a perfect day for a drive.

"Where do you want to go?" Emma asked.

"Let's just ride," I suggested. "We'll end up wherever the car takes us."

Emma agreed, going for her coat.

"Let's bring the dogs," I added. "They love the car." "*Both* dogs?" she asked, surprised.

"Absolutely. We can't leave one home alone." I busied myself putting on Sarge's leash, certain I was avoiding Emma's suspicious stare.

We piled into the car and I kept a leisurely speed on my way to Ellenville, New York.

Ellenville is a small village in the Rondout Valley at the base of the Catskills.

It has a picturesque main street perfect for an afternoon stroll.

"Look," I said offhandedly, pointing down a side street. "Isn't that the shingle for Esme the Psychic?" I saw the sign, emblazoned *"Psychic Readings. Walk-Ins Welcome."*

"It is," she agreed.

"Did you want to stop in? Maybe she can give you a reading," I suggested.

Nuff said.

The Psychic Shop sold crystals, candles, incense, and New Agey staples. It was a whole new world of scents for Sarge and Evil. We looked around for Esme.

"You came for your reading!" she said, coming from the back room to greet us.

Emma was amazed. "How did she know?" she whispered.

"I guess she's the real deal," I answered, trying to sound just as surprised.

"Come in and take a seat," Esme invited. "Feel free to record our conversation. Sometimes there is so much to process, it becomes impossible to remember."

We went to our chairs and before I could say "sit," Sarge was already stretched out on the floor. "Sit," I told Evil. She remained standing.

"Sit," Emma repeated. Evil sat.

Esme inspected the four of us, one by one, as if she were about to guess our weight. Sarge whimpered, got up and walked back toward the door, and lay down there instead, perhaps to make his departure seem more imminent. At last, Esme's eyes fell upon Evil and stayed there.

Emma finally broke the silence. "Her name's 'Evie,'" she offered.

Esme shook her head. "No. That's not her name. It's the name you call her."

You're right, I thought. *It's really "Evil."*

"She doesn't have the soul of a dog. She has the soul of a ten-year-old boy." Esme focused again on Evil.

"Tell me your name, child."

"Damian?" I offered.

Esme ignored me. "His name is Toby; he was born on an Indiana farm in 1846. Go on, Toby."

She leaned forward, prompting Evil to walk toward her. Their faces were less than a foot apart.

"Toby had a terrible death," she continued. "He holds his father accountable."

"Why?" I asked.

"His father wanted to punish him. Toby left the gate to the farm's stockade open and their horses ran away. His father chased him with a horse whip."

"Well, in the 1800s that was probably a valid reason for a little whipping."

Both Esme and Emma gaped at me. Reflexively, I had bonded with the father.

"Let's pretend my husband's not here," Emma suggested.

"Toby ran into the barn and hid in the hayloft," Esme continued. "When his father came after him, he tried to climb out of the window they lifted the hay in through. He lost his footing. That's the last thing he remembers. Until you."

Evil sat fixed at attention, rapt.

"That's horrible," Emma said, kneeling beside Evil and hugging her. "The poor boy. You poor dog!"

"Poor us," I added.

"Poor *us*?" Emma repeated, "This dog—I mean, boy— met a horrible end and you're feeling sorry for yourself?"

"It was a horrible end, yes, and the kid didn't deserve it," I continued. "Did they lose all their horses?"

Esme looked at Evil, but Evil's attention was on me. "Not that it matters!" I quickly added. "But you're just hearing Toby's side of the story."

"You're not actually taking his father's side, are you?" Emma asked.

I didn't answer, pressing Esme instead. "You believe this dog has the spirit of a boy who died over a hundred years ago. Reincarnation."

"That's right," Esme agreed.

"So the boy went from being a human being to a dog. Isn't that a step down? It's not like coming back as a mushroom, but doesn't that mean Toby's soul had a lot of karmic catching up to do?"

"What are you saying, Mark?" Emma snapped.

"We know nothing about Toby but the fact he died as he was about to be punished. So he says." I pointed to Evil. "But what if we're being conned?"

Esme crossed her arms. "This is what he told me." "I'm not arguing that. I'm saying that's *only* what he told you. For all we know, he could have been a gang leader terrorizing the town. Bullying, vandalizing, starting a protection racket."

"He was ten years old," Emma reminded me.

I saw no bottom to the grave I was digging. "For all we know, he could also have been a Mongol warlord in another life, or a cannibal thrown out of his tribe for bad behavior."

Esme stopped me. "Your point?"

"What this dog did in the past doesn't matter. In the present, Evil has dedicated her life to making mine miserable, and it has to stop."

"Evil?'" Esme asked Emma.

"Don't go there," my wife cautioned.

"Why does this dog hate me?"

"Does she hate men?" Esme wondered.

"Not at all," Emma answered.

"Exactly!" I agreed. "So why me? I'm not the one who chased her into the barn with a whip!"

"Unless you're Toby's reincarnated father," Emma offered.

"The farmer? Me? Slopping pigs, castrating cattle? You can't be serious! I've never even had a garden!" I looked at Esme, desperate to address the reason we were here. "We made this appointment because we hoped you could tell us something useful about this dog's behavior."

"Stop there. This is something you scheduled in advance?" Emma interrupted.

"Yes." Esme answered before I could. "And if we're finished here, you can pay by cash or credit."

"Have you ever asked yourself why Evie has problems with only you?" Emma confronted me. "People love dogs. Dogs love people. Don't you ever wonder what went wrong here?"

"I don't need to wonder," I responded. "What went wrong was you adopting this dog without even telling me about it!"

"So you're angry that I made a decision on my own?" she shot back.

"It's a decision that impacts both our lives!"

"Every choice you have ever made in your career impacted our lives," Emma stated. "Your deadlines, your travel, your time away. How many times in the last few years have you consulted me before making up your own mind about any of it?"

"We've been married thirty-two years," I said. "Don't you think by now I know how'd you react without having to ask you?"

"No," Emma answered in a low tone. "I don't think you have a clue." She took Evil's leash and thanked Esme. "I'll be outside," she announced. As she was leaving, Evil looked back at me with an expression I'd never seen before. If I didn't know better, I would say it was pity.

I picked up Sarge's leash. "What about him?" I asked Esme. "Can you tell me anything about him?"

She took a brief look. "He's a dog." Sarge didn't seem upset hearing it.

"In case you don't realize it, your marriage is over," Esme said when I paid her.

A sardonic psychic, I thought. "Thank you. Is there an additional charge?"

She shook her head. "You don't have to be psychic to know that."

"No one would think of bringing a dog into a church."
Virginia Woolf, *Jacob's Room*

CHAPTER ELEVEN

EVIL AND JESUS

On Halloween night, Emma invited our friends, Frank and Stephanie, to dinner. Frank is my oldest friend. We sat together at the same kindergarten table in Sacred Heart Grammar School when we were five. On the first day, I proudly wore my Mickey Mouse watch, hoping everyone was suitably impressed. "Do you know how to tell time?" he asked, suspicious. That led to my humiliation and a lifelong bond.

Frank and Stephanie were one of the few couples with whom we socialized who were married as long as we were. Early on, the four of us privately placed bets on the longevity of other couples in our circle. Fallout began as early as year one with Daisy and David Gleason. Daisy said she had no choice—she was allergic to David. This was suspicious for two reasons. One, we had never seen Daisy even sniffle when she and David were together. The second sign was David's quitting his job at a prestigious law firm, moving to Key West, and sharing a house with Sebastian, nearly twenty-five years his junior. David said he and Sebastian planned to open a law office together. The last time we heard from David was a Christmas card with a photo of him and Sebastian in bathing suits, surfing with Santa, not a courtroom in sight.

On the flip side of our marriage forecasts was the deceptively genial competition between Frank and Stephanie, Emma and me, to see which couple would be married the longest. Rules were agreed upon. Divorce was inconceivable, but if either couple separated yet somehow ended up back together, their days apart would be deducted from their final total. The competition ended with the death of any of the four of us.

Left unsaid was that the widow or widower would be congratulating the winning couple at a funeral parlor.

Charlie screeched "Hola!" at the sight of our friends, then began imitating a phone ringing non-stop. I rolled his cage into a dark room, where I hoped he would sleep. Sarge was already napping under the dining room table, and Evil, on her best behavior with guests, sat pertly before them and pretended to be the dog they praised.

"What a good dog!" Frank said as he petted her.

"You're so beautiful!" Stephanie praised, leaning down to face Evil as if she could lip-read.

I had been warned by Emma not to bad-mouth Evil and, most especially, not to call her "Evil." She needn't have bothered. With Evil putting on a performance of such innocence she might have been mistaken for Bambi, any complaints would leave me looking like the hunter who shot his mother.

As we passed around the serving plate of flank steak, I made sure Evil's eyes were on me as I bit into my first cut, relishing it as if it were the last slice of beef on the planet. I could see her self-control waver, but she was not about to break character as Wonder Dog and show her true colors.

Names of favorite Halloween movies were being offered up around the table. *"House on Haunted Hill," "Silence of the Lambs," "Rosemary's Baby."*

"What about you?" Stephanie asked me. "What's the scariest movie you ever saw?" I thought about it. As a kid, after seeing it at the Rivoli Theater five times with my parents, the idea of viewing *The Sound of Music* even once more frightened the hell out of me at eleven and still does today.

The ring of our doorbell stopped me from answering. I went to answer it, picking up the plastic pumpkin we had filled with chocolate bars. I was convinced their rocket-high sugar content was capable of corroding any metal objects that might be concealed in any neighborhood apples.

Opening the front door, I faced two sullen boys without apparent costumes. They were in their awkward early teens; perhaps they felt too mature to put on a costume yet couldn't give up the prospect of free candy.

"Who are you guys dressed as?" I asked, dropping candy into each bag.

"Kids who forgot their costumes," the tallest answered. Both waited to see if I'd laugh or take back their chocolate.

A loud bark startled all of us. Standing at my side was Evil, ears pinned back. Unnerved, the boys began to walk backwards in retreat as Evil began to snarl.

What was happening? Was Evil guarding her home, sensing trouble and coming to protect me? *Me? No. There had to be another reason.*

Then I saw it—a chocolate wrapper lay chewed up on the floor at my feet. *The chocolate.* Unseen by us, Evil must have eaten a bar of chocolate. I knew that chocolate contains a stimulant, theobromine, that affects a dog's central nervous system. It could cause seizures, potentially fatal ones. Even as these facts flashed through my mind, I realized I was facing a moral dilemma. Possible seizures. *Should I run for the car keys and race with Evil to the nearest veterinarian or should I just return to our dinner, hoping that for me, Christmas had come early this year?*

By now the teen duo had reached the sidewalk and, having received both tricks and treats, broke into a run. Evil didn't turn her head to watch them go, but still stared ahead, her snarl growing to a growl.

I looked in the direction Evil faced. Walking toward us was a man holding the hand of his young son, dressed as some superhero.

Evil began to bark again, even louder than before. Did Evil have issues with Marvel Comics or was she a stockholder in DC?

No, it wasn't the boy she was barking at. It was his father, dressed as a Father. A Catholic priest.

A movie image came to me then, the film's first scene showing Father Merrin approaching a large stone statue in the desert. The sculpture was of a gruesome creature constructed with assorted animal limbs. It stared with hatred at Merrin, who suddenly became aware of the howls of dogs fighting tooth and claw behind him.

"The Exorcist!" I said aloud, returning to the table.

"Scared the hell out of me as a kid," Frank said.

"An exorcism," I suddenly realized. "That's just what she needs. An exorcism!"

"An exorcism?" Stephanie repeated.

"Who is 'she'?" Frank asked, anticipating a laugh line.

"Evil!" I told him, looking at the dog before me. Both Frank and Stephanie regarded me with disbelief.

"Evie? Why would you call her Evil?" Stephanie asked.

Emma leaned on the table, covering her face with her hands.

"I'll tell you why," I began, unable to stop myself. As I began to list Evil's war crimes, the dog went to Emma's chair and stretched out beside it, fully at ease. She knew well that I'd be sleeping on the couch again tonight while she shared our king-size bed with my wife.

Once we'd said our good nights and seen Frank and Stephanie to the door, I braced myself for whatever Emma would throw at me.

"Have you made an appointment with a counselor yet?" I hesitated, realizing that she was asking about a marriage counselor, not a dog behavior therapist.

"I will. Tomorrow."

"I really hope so," she said, her final words for the night.

In truth, I was hoping we wouldn't need any counseling at all after tomorrow.

The next morning, I headed to a Catholic church only three blocks away, comforted to find its name was St. Francis. Was it just a coincidence or, finally, a sign of divine, animal-friendly intervention?

Evil walked easily beside me. For a change, she didn't run ahead to the end of her leash, straining my every muscle as if she were pulling me like a sled. Keeping me off balance was routine for Evil, as was radically changing direction to unexpectedly charge through tall, thick hedges. This gave me two options: following her through the barbed briars where I would emerge, gashed and bleeding, to see Evil unscathed, or letting go of her leash and hoping to catch her when she reappeared.

By now, Evil knew I would never let go of her leash. I had tried that only once. A year ago, when she had charged into a copse of rose bushes, she took the last of my patience. That time, releasing Evil's tether had released in me a burst of euphoria. Maybe she would keep running, crossing city and even state lines. I reproached myself only for not removing her dog tags, which disclosed our address and phone number.

But at that moment, I was determined to enjoy a life free of Evil. On my way home I concocted a number of accounts to prove to Emma I had had no alternative but to drop the end of her dog's leash. Discarding my first excuse that I had had a mini-stroke, I settled on a story that wouldn't call for a follow-up cat scan and MRI.

What I decided on was this: Evil had spotted a squirrel and bolted after it with such super canine speed that her leash was yanked from my grasp, leaving me with the equivalent of a rope burn. I rubbed dirt on my right hand, squeezed some red choke-cherries from a shrub I was passing, then tied my handkerchief around my instant injury and started home.

A block away I could see Evil seated on the front porch, looking back for me. If she had been another kind of dog, she would have waited patiently for me to get there, when I would take her leash and we could enter together as if our walk had been uneventful. Instead, she gave out a mournful yowl that immediately drew Emma to the door. Seeing her distraught dog so pitifully alone, she threw open the door and knelt to embrace her. She was still fussing when I arrived moments later.

"What happened?" Emma demanded, not waiting for an answer. "Do you see how frightened she is? How many times did I say you had to wrap the end of the leash around your hand so you couldn't lose her? It's like you let it go on purpose."

"I didn't," I protested, holding out my "bloody" hand. Emma gave it a look.

"Are you bleeding berries?" she asked, picking off a tiny berry skin.

Evil simpered.

"It's all right, Evie," Emma soothed her. "You're going to get a treat. How about a Doggie Konz?" Doggie Konz were small paper ice cream cones for dogs that Evil inhaled in seconds.

"Oh, I forgot," Emma continued. "We're out of Konz. Mark, will you run down to the market for them?"

"Why don't I find her rawhide stick and give her that instead?" I suggested.

Emma turned from Evil to me, her tone no longer comforting.

"Pick up a few boxes. And a bag of Blue Buffalo," she said, referring to a high-end dog food that was more expensive than a twelve pack of Coors Light. Emma turned back to Evil, her voice soothing. "You've had such a stressful day, sweetie, haven't you?"

Evil licked Emma's face. It was a behavior I most abhorred, so Evil licked me as often as given the opportunity.

But now, on our way to St. Francis, Evil was suspiciously compliant, her pace matching mine. I watched her as the church came into view, slightly disappointed that she wasn't projectile vomiting or bursting into flames. By the time I rang the rectory's doorbell she was even wagging her tail.

A white-haired man in polo shirt and black slacks answered the door. He was in his late seventies, and his severe, black-framed glasses were a contrast to his pleasant smile.

"Can I help you?" he asked.

"I'm looking for Monsignor Becton." "You've found him, son."

I gave him my name and mentioned we were neighbors. "I was hoping I could speak with you about a particular church rite." The Monsignor agreed, saying he had an appointment in half an hour, but we could talk until then. He invited me in, saying I could leave my dog in the rectory's backyard.

"It's totally fenced," he offered. "He'll be perfectly safe."

"He's a she. And, if it's not too much trouble, I'd like to keep her with me."

A slight frown. "Are you sight-challenged?"

"No, Monsignor. My sight is fine."

"Is your dog a therapy animal?"

"Not per se. But she has put me back into therapy."

Somewhat reluctant, the Monsignor stepped aside to let us enter. I suspected the fact that I had a St. in my last name gave me clerical street cred.

"What a beautiful dog," the Monsignor observed. Evil gazed up in faux adoration as he stroked her smooth, gleaming coat. "Come into my office. Would you like some tea or coffee?"

"No thank you," I replied, eager to get down to business.

"Well, I'd be a terrible host if I didn't offer your dog water. What's her name?"

"Evie," I said. Evil would come later. When the Monsignor disappeared into his kitchen, Evil looked at me, smiling on the inside. To her, this was a game of cat and mouse, with me playing rodent.

"I'm more of a cat person," the Monsignor said, returning with a bowl and placing it beside his desk. "But Evie seems like a very special dog."

"That she is," I agreed.

He watched Evil lap furiously at the water until it was gone.

"She must have been very thirsty."

"I doubt that, Monsignor. She just wanted to make you think I was in the habit of dehydrating her."

He checked to see if I was serious, then frowned, looking at Evil's angelic innocence, then back to me.

"I don't think I understand. Why don't you tell me the reason you're here?" he finally asked.

I pointed. "She's the reason."

He was confused. "We have the Blessing of the Animals on October 4th, St. Francis' feast day. But if you like, I have no problem blessing Evie now."

"She needs more than a blessing," I told him. "You were right. This is no ordinary dog. She's incredibly cunning, deliberately destructive, and vindictive."

"Oh?"

"There's something in her that's despised me from the beginning. And to be honest, that loathing is reciprocal. Our relationship is adversarial to the point of perversity."

"Perversity?" He sounded alarmed.

"Not bestiality," I said to his obvious relief. "I'm talking about premeditated bad behavior. We've gone through trainers like paper towels. They tried obedience training, behavioral training, clicker and electroshock training. One trainer quit the business, another retired early. The first trainer we had is now training seals."

Evil began wagging her tail.

"I can see how upsetting this is to you," the Monsignor acknowledged. "But I don't know why you've come to me."

I hesitated, making sure my voice was under control, and tried to sound as sensible as I could.

"I believe this dog is possessed," I told him.

For a few moments I listened to the tick of his wall clock.

"Is this some sort of prank?" He sounded testy.

"If only it was," I answered.

"You truly believe that this this friendly, quite adorable dog is possessed by the devil?"

"I do. I think that pound for pound, there's more devil than dog in there. Monsignor, we need an exorcist."

Evie had turned onto her back, inviting the Monsignor to rub her belly.

He smiled. "Mr. St. Germain, the topic of exorcism is a very sensitive one in the Catholic Church. I promise you that there are far fewer cases of possession in our world than there are movies about them. Exorcisms must be sanctioned by a bishop, and that is only after there is a thorough examination that precludes the possibility of mental illness. This is a very serious, potentially dangerous matter."

"I couldn't agree more," I said. "I'm happy to meet with anyone to answer questions and kickstart the investigation." "Let me be direct. An exorcism is a sacramental rite of the Church to be employed on human beings, not animals." "I disagree, Monsignor." I pulled out my phone, calling up the file of information I had researched. "Jesus was an animal exorcist."

"What?"

"Mark 5:1–20. Jesus comes upon a man possessed by demons. The demons beg Jesus not to destroy them but, instead, send them into a herd of nearby pigs. Jesus does that, exorcising the demons by zapping them into the swine, and tops that miracle by causing the demonic pigs to throw themselves off a convenient cliff to drown in the sea."

"I know the passage," the Monsignor said. "But Jesus exorcised the man, not the pigs. Animals are animals; there is nothing supernatural or otherworldly about them."

I consulted my iPhone Bible notes. "Wouldn't you say that there was something otherworldly about Balaam's donkey? Numbers 22:21–39. 'Then the Lord opened the donkey's mouth and it said to Balaam, "What have I done to you to make you beat me these three times?"' Then, Balaam and the jackass had a huge dust-up, and even God put in his two cents.

"And what about the prophet Elisha and the bears?" I pressed on.

"There are no talking bears in the Bible," he interrupted. "2 Kings 2:23–24. Elisha is leaving the city when he runs into a gang of smart-ass kids who start calling him 'Baldy.' Elisha curses them in the name of the Lord, and before you could say 'oops,' two giant bears bolt out of the woods and tear the kids to pieces, all forty-two of them."

I noticed Evie had turned her attention to me. She was enjoying the story.

"So, whether the bears were possessed by demons or God was in a bad mood, it's another case of animal possession. This all comes from the Good Book, Monsignor. Not the *National Enquirer*."

The Monsignor looked at his watch and I knew my time to make my point was running out.

"I'm afraid we have to cut this short. If I'm five minutes late for our tee time, I have to give up my slot at the club," he said, rising.

"Are you telling me your golf game has priority over demonic possession?" I countered, my frustration growing. "I need advice. I don't know where else to turn."

I pointed to Evil, now yawning.

"Look at her!" I implored Monsignor Becton. "Don't you see that? She's mocking me! She has sucked every ounce of goodwill out of me. Dear God, Monsignor! What the hell can I do to stop Evil?"

Pause. "Evil? You call your dog Evil?"

Caught. Major setback. "So does the trainer at World O' Pups," I defended myself.

"You asked me for advice, so my advice is this—seek a psychiatrist. The sooner the better."

"A dog psychiatrist? Been there, done that."

"Not for your dog. For you." He opened his office door and patted Evil as she walked past him. "Mr. St. Germain, you'll be in my prayers. And I'm happy, at any time, to hear your confession. Goodbye, now."

Wordless, all defenses drained, I slunk to the front door, where Evil was waiting to walk me home.

"Who let the dogs out / Woof woof woof woof woof."
Baha Men, "Who Let the Dogs Out"

CHAPTER TWELVE

EVIL AND THE APOCALYPSE

I looked at the clock and realized I had been sitting at my desk for ten hours. It was now seven o'clock, long past our usual dinner time. Normally, I would finish at five, take a walk in the yard to clear my head, then head into the kitchen, where I would usually find Emma cooking dinner. She's a terrific cook, while I'm skillful at takeout.

At some point early in our marriage, Emma and I had agreed on a schedule. I'd write in the morning, we'd have lunch together if she could make it home from her counseling office, and I'd knock off work at five so we could spend time together before sitting down to eat.

I had promised myself after my last job working for someone else that it was my last nine-to-five position. To keep that promise, I vowed I would write nine to five. A screenplay, teleplay, or play in the morning, a short lunch, and then a second project or rewrites after lunch.

I didn't lock myself into my home office. The door was always open. With our children, Martin and Becca, I wanted to be accessible at any time. If Abraham Lincoln let his children run in and out of the Oval Office, how could I pretend that any challenges writing a half-hour sitcom stacked up to a civil war?

On this night, when I had worked until seven, I braced myself as I left my desk. Whether Emma would be disappointed, annoyed, or silent, it would be justified. I had broken my promise by working late once again.

I petted Sarge on my way to find Emma and said "Hello, Charlie" to our parrot, who responded, as always, "Hello, Charlie." No Evil in sight, I noticed as I picked up the mail on the table by the front door. Bills, offers to trim trees or pave the driveway, and a large brown envelope. A quick look through everything else, always hopeful for checks, but there weren't any.

The brown envelope, stiffened by cardboard inside it, had a name and return address on it that I didn't recognize. Maybe a photo, I thought, though I didn't expect any. The letter inside was even more unexpected.

Mr. St. Germain,

I don't know if you'll remember me. I saw your play Freud's Last Session at New World Stages in New York City. When I met you after the talkback, I told you that I had sat on Sigmund Freud's lap when I was six years old. My father, a friend of the doctor, had dropped a book off for Freud at his London address, bringing me along. The only memory of Dr. Freud I have today is that his beard was such a bright white.

I'm moving in with my daughter, who you also met, and in packing came across a letter to my father that I thought you might enjoy. Please accept it as a thank you gift for a wonderful night at the theater.

   Sincerely,

   Evelyn Katz

At the bottom of the large brown envelope was a small letter-sized white one. Opening it, I couldn't make out the letter's content, written in German. But the letterhead, "Prof. Dr. Freud," and his signature were as distinct as if it had been posted yesterday.

I was past stunned. I don't remember walking into the kitchen holding the letter and the rest of the mail. Emma was at the table with a magazine. Without a word I put Freud's letter before her.

Whatever feelings she had about my being late were forgotten. We hugged, cheered, poured a glass of wine, and opened a beer, toasting Evelyn Katz. Overwhelmed, I sat down at the table and blathered on as one of the envelopes I brought in caught Emma's eye.

"Who is Dr. Leah McShane?" she asked as she opened it. "This is a bill for therapy. I don't understand. We haven't even gone to therapy yet."

As joyful as I'd felt a moment ago was as stricken as I felt now. How could I tell Emma that I had seen a therapist for Evil's behavior and totally forgotten about contacting a marriage counselor?

"Dog behavior therapist?" She looked up from the bill in disbelief. "You went to a therapist to talk about Evie?"

"I thought it would be good for all of us."

"For you, you mean. Oh my God, she charged this much?"

"I'll find a marriage counselor tomorrow," I said, but she had already left the room.

In the living room, Emma was putting on her coat. "Emma, wait. Can we talk?"

"Why start now? I'm going to take a walk."

"Please. I know how upset you are. I should have found a marriage counselor immediately."

"But you didn't. Because, deep down, you didn't want to."

"You're right, I really didn't," I admitted. "I think we can work things out without getting someone else involved."

"You haven't even admitted we have a problem. You want to sweep it under the rug, lock yourself in your room to work, and think of nothing else. No. I'm wrong. You think about Evie and blame her for everything from our problems to global warming."

I hesitated, contemplating a link between Evil and melting polar ice.

"You're right," I agreed. "It's completely my fault. But I can change, and I will."

"Will you?"

"Yes! And I'll prove it to you. Really. Just give me another chance."

Emma looked at me, thinking a thousand unspoken thoughts. Finally, she took off her coat.

"Thank you," I said. She allowed herself to be slightly kissed. "Let me do dinner," I offered, feeling magnanimous.

"Does that mean Chinese, Mexican, or pizza?" she asked, softening.

"How about a smorgasbord?" I offered as we returned to the kitchen. "I can even—"

I stopped. The mail was still on the table—with the exception of Freud's letter.

I panicked. "It's gone! Freud's letter! It was right here!"

"Are you sure?" Emma sorted through the mail. "Did you put it in your pocket?"

"No. Definitely not." I looked under the table. Nothing. "It has to be here. No one took it."

"Evil!" I shouted at the top of my lungs.

"You don't know that!"

"Evil!" I bellowed again.

"Take a breath. We'll go find her."

"She's chewed up Freud like she chewed up Yoko!"

"Why would she take that letter and not the others?"

"Because it made me happy! Her purpose in life is to make mine miserable! I'm tired of it!"

"Mark, take a breath. You don't even know she's responsible."

"I'm tired of you standing up for her all the time too!" By now I was ranting.

"Don't yell at me!"

"I'm not!" I yelled.

"Is this your big change?" Emma shouted back. "This is what you promised?"

"She's truly evil!" I insisted. "Why don't you see it?"

"Really? Did the dog therapist diagnose her as 'evil'?"

"Not exactly," I hedged. "But I didn't bring her with me."

"You talked about Evie behind her back?" Emma said, incredulous.

"Yes! Because you don't believe me! I had to talk to someone! That dog's fiendish! She's duped everybody but me all along! She conned you the same as she did that priest."

Silence.

"What priest?"

How could I have said that? And having said it, how could I now avoid an answer? I prayed for a heart attack or a meteor through the roof. If the earth would only cooperate by opening under me, I would have been a happy man.

There was no right thing to say. And so I said the worst thing, the most lethal five words I could have spoken. "It's the dog or me."

The rest of the night is fragmented in my memory. Arguments. Tears. Sarge hiding under the kitchen table and Charlie, for once, silent. Taking a suitcase from the attic and going into the bedroom to pack. Evil. Standing on the bed. Waiting. In front of her, resting on the bedspread, was the letter from Sigmund Freud. I grabbed it, inspected it. No teeth marks. No drool. It was in the same shape it was when I pulled it from its envelope.

I stared at Evil and she stared back.

"You beat me," I conceded. "*Veni, vidi, vici.* You came, you saw, you conquered."

She stretched out on my side of the bed, a bed I somehow knew I would never sleep in again. In a house I would never live in again. Thirty-two years of marriage plus the three of dating; a thirty-five-year relationship brought to a close in eleven months of Evil.

"Well played, dog. Well played." Evil yawned.

"Not the least hard thing to bear when they go from us,
these quiet friends, is that they carry away with them
so many years of our own lives."
John Galsworthy

CHAPTER THIRTEEN

SARGE

Because I didn't want to see them, the signs of his aging had to announce themselves dramatically. Stairs were his first problem. Since the back door had five steep ones, it was easy not to think about it and simply bring him in at the ground level front door instead.

It became impossible for Sarge to climb up onto the couch, and he ignored a ramp I purchased. Then, climbing stairs to the second floor to my bedroom became out of the question, and Sarge slept on his dog bed in the kitchen.

I stopped using my office, also on the second floor. To keep Sarge company, I'd work downstairs at the kitchen table. More and more of his day was spent sleeping. Sarge was the only dog in the house at this point, with Evie/Evil living with Emma, my former wife, in Woodstock.

When my daughter, Becca, returned from Thailand with her own rescue puppy, Leonard, the younger dog was excited to find a playmate. Sarge didn't share his excitement. He allowed Leonard to play all around him but didn't join in the fun. Chasing a ball or a stick was for kids.

Sarge's walk slowed, then he seemed less sure on his feet. He showed no pain, but he was less energetic by the day. When I brought him to Berkshires veterinarian Nancy Iverson, she gave Sarge vitamins. When I returned, pressing to know what else could be done, Dr. Iverson shook her head. "You can't cure old age," she told me. As Sarge was a rescue, we never knew his exact age. When we adopted him, we were told he was three or four years old. He lived with us for eleven years, so whether he was fourteen or fifteen, he had a long life for a Labrador retriever, whose life span is usually between eleven and twelve.

I didn't want to hear it. I continued to bring him in to be checked but received the same prognosis.

"When it's time," Dr. Iverson finally told me, "you can bring him in and be with him when we help him go to sleep." *No*, I told myself. *That's not going to happen. He'll get stronger. We have years left.*

"We" was how I thought of it, not "he."

In Sarge's last two weeks, he stopped eating. He got up only to slowly walk outside to relieve himself, and his breathing became labored. I sat on the floor with him midweek, giving him pep talks and petting him constantly. I refused to recognize that recovery was impossible but finally had to face the fact that I was being selfish. I practiced making the call to Dr. Iverson without filling up, then made it. She told me I could bring Sarge in the next day.

At the first sight of him the next morning, I burst into tears. I knelt by him until it was time for our appointment. Still crying, I picked Sarge up with difficulty, carried him to the porch, pushed open its screen door, and walked through the garden toward the car.

Sarge was always happy to get into the car for a ride. In his later years he needed to be helped up, but he was always game for looking out the window and inhaling the world of scents rushing past his nose.

His last trips had been only to the vet. Sarge accepted that. That morning, seeing the car ahead, Sarge began thrashing in my arms so powerfully that I had no choice but to put him down. Once on his feet, he ran back to the house with a speed that amazed me. I opened the door; he went back to his bed, lay down, and looked up at me. He had made himself clear. He knew, somehow, that it would be his last trip anywhere and refused. Sarge wanted to die at home.

For two more days he hung on. I would look at him and wonder how he could have gotten so gray without me seeing, or not wanting to see it. Early on the second night, Sarge got up and walked slowly to the rear porch of the house that led to the yard. He stopped on the porch, where he could see the yard and stream through the glass. Soon, he slept.

I stretched out on the floor beside him but left the room often so that I could cry where he couldn't hear me. In the middle of the night, I was physically and emotionally exhausted and decided to rest on my bed, only for a few minutes.

When I awoke, I saw that more than minutes had gone by. It was morning, and I knew Sarge was gone before I touched him, petting him for the last time.

I won't forgive myself for not staying by his side.

"Evil never dies."
Stephen King, *"Cujo"*

CHAPTER FOURTEEN

EVIL REDUX

Evil and I don't see much of each other anymore since the divorce. I can't say it was amicable for anyone but her. I took custody of Sarge and Charlie. Sarge seemed grateful for the dog divorce. Once, Evil had seemed to love him in her way, but that love had died. She had been riding him, and even drawn blood. I could swear Sarge trembled with relief as he left our former home.

Several months after moving to my new home in Massachusetts, I got a call from Emma. A friend was sick; she had to fly out to Indiana that night but had just gotten a call from Evil's pet sitter backing out.

She gave me a chance to say something witty or disparaging. I didn't, but in that moment I realized how desperate she was, having to call and ask a favor.

"I can't keep her here," I explained. "Becca is visiting with her dog." The last time Evil had seen Leonard, she'd eyed him like the last shrimp taco on a party tray.

"Okay," Emma said. "Thanks anyway."

"Have you tried everyone?"

"Do you really think you were at the top of my list?"

I laughed. She laughed. Charlie, from his cage in my office, laughed.

"I'll work this out," I told Emma. "Don't miss your plane."

Knowing Emma would be away for a week, I looked online for a dog sitter. There were websites devoted to all things canine: people who would feed, walk, or even board your pet in a room furnished with its own television.

It was Doggie Dale who caught my eye. Five-star reviews and impressive testimonials. Doggie Dale had a small house nearby Emma's, a fenced-in yard, and two dogs of his own. He was a heavy, officious man with a flushed face and a crooked little toupee; I guessed him to be in his late fifties. I wondered if he took up boarding because he loved dogs or so he might afford a better wig. In his living room, Dale had a chest full of dog toys for them to play with and a Game Boy for himself. Dale complained about the dog food I brought with me and insisted I return with only organic provisions. I was about to protest, but his face flushed redder and I didn't want to lose him before the week was out.

Annoyed, I returned with Dale approved chow and waved goodbye to Evil, who ignored me.

At 11:45 that night, Dale called, shouting into the phone that I get "that monster" out of his home immediately. I reluctantly got in the car and drove to his home, wondering all the while if Evil had swallowed one of Dale's dogs, his game controller, or his wig.

Still seething, Dale let me in. He swore Evil took pleasure in tormenting him. She had chased the other dogs around the house, tried to escape the yard by digging under the fence, and, by yanking the internet cables, caused the television to crash to the ground and disable the Game Boy.

Now, Evil was at his front screen door, jumping up against it, desperate to get out. She looked at me, defiant but shamed. She needed me, and we both knew it.

"I've never met any dog like this one," Dale fumed. "I don't know what you can do, but for the love of God, you'd better do something."

"Actually," I told him, "I don't have to 'do' anything. She's my ex-wife's dog."

"Your ex-wife's? Really?" he replied, mumbling the rest. "I wonder why that marriage went south."

Hearing the sound of a ripping screen, we both looked at the door. Evil had jumped through it.

I ran out to the porch and looked up and down the block. No sign of Evil. Nothing but night.

I walked down the driveway to the car as Dale called from his front door.

"Good luck! Maybe you'll never find her!"

I can't say that there wasn't a part of me that agreed with him, but I was surprised at the other feelings I had as well. Dread, thinking of the call I'd have to make, telling Emma her dog had run away. Sadness, imagining the pain she'd feel; the same pain as I felt losing Sarge.

And, lastly, concern. Evil as she may be, she was running through a dark, rural area full of cars that might hit her and surrounded by woods where bears and coyotes could do worse.

I reached the car and walked around to the driver's side. There, sitting only feet away, was Evil. I stopped and we stared at each other. *What was she feeling?* A spot of gratitude, having been rescued from the loud man with crooked hair? A grudging realization that if she wanted to eat this week, it made no sense to bite the hand that would feed her?

Or was it rope-a-dope once again? When I walked toward her, would she sprint to a distance where she'd eagerly wait for me to try and be fooled again?

I opened the driver's door and looked at her. Slowly, she walked toward me, then jumped in. I slid into the driver's seat, prepared to push Evil far enough away that I could get a good grip on the steering wheel, anticipating that Evil would move to her usual intrusive front seat position, her nose pressed against the windshield.

But she wasn't there. I turned around to see her stretched out on the back seat, her tail beating the cushions, impatient … happy?

I started the car. She didn't move. For that short time it took to drive home, Evil and I were at peace.

SPECIAL THANKS to my Woodstock Writers Group, John Bowers, Nina Shengold, Zachary Sklar, David Smilow, and Mary Louise Wilson, for offering welcomed suggestions and support, and, especially, to Laura Cunningham, who expertly and patiently led me from draft to publication.

ABOUT THE AUTHOR

Mark St. Germain has written for film, television, and the stage. His plays include *Freud's Last Session*, *Camping with Henry and Tom*, *Becoming Dr. Ruth*, *Dancing Lessons*, and *Eleanor*. He co-wrote Carroll Ballard's Warner Brothers film *Duma* and directed the documentary *MY DOG: An Unconditional Love Story*. Mark is an Associate Artist at the Barrington Stage Company, where a theater is named for him.

Cover Design by Jace Chloe

Made in the USA
Middletown, DE
24 August 2021